Waiting
and
Dating

An Orthodox Christian Guide for Navigating
Singleness and Godly Relationships

LILYAN ANDREWS

ANCIENT FAITH PUBLISHING

CHESTERTON, INDIANA

Published by:
Ancient Faith Publishing
A Division of Ancient Faith Ministries
1050 Broadway, Suite 6
Chesterton, IN 46304

Unless otherwise noted, Scripture quotations are taken from the New
King James Version, © 1979, 1980, 1982 by Thomas Nelson, Inc. Used
by permission.

Cover silhouettes via amingdesign/Shutterstock.com
Cover design and interior illustrations by Samuel Heble

ISBN: 978-1-955890-37-3

Library of Congress Control Number: 2024941839

Waiting and Dating is a timely and rewarding book: The reward comes in the form of liberating insights about the real world of real dating. For young people, and for older people trying to help them, this book can be a luminous beacon. Lilyan writes clearly and convincingly, and her book might be best summed up with her own words, "We need to keep in mind that the fundamental goal of marriage is holiness, not temporary happiness." I highly recommend *Waiting and Dating* as a guide through the turbulent waters of the cultural dating scene.

—**Albert S. Rossi**, PhD, Clinical Psychologist

Dating can be such a confusing time, full of both uncertainty and exhilaration. While dating, we often struggle to let our faith serve as our firm foundation. In this book, we find not only a helpful guide to dating but the spiritual wisdom we need to make choices that transcend cultural tides and help us honor God as we navigate one of the most important decisions we make in adulthood.

—**Dr. Roxanne K. Louh**, PsyD, Licensed Psychologist,
coauthor of *Renewing You* and *6 Hours, 7 Lessons*

We've suffered through so many dating books that never gave us a full and balanced understanding of purity, dating, and marriage in a Christian context. Lilyan's book puts an end to this, offering a clear-cut, balanced, and theologically sound Christian road map to pure relationships that lead to holy marriages. She clearly debunks some huge myths about dating, sex, and marriage that still prevail, but with a warm heart and a kind tone that invite her readers to seek something better—the holy lives, whether married or single, that God desires for us. I'm so thankful I'll be able to hand this book to my own children when they start asking questions about dating!

—**Phoebe Farag Mikhail**, author of *Putting Joy into Practice*

I am grateful for Lilyan Andrews and her voice in the Coptic Orthodox community, encouraging healthy relationships and having the courage to discuss issues that are often dismissed or ignored! If you are looking to get healthy and engage in healthy dating, her book is an important resource!

—**Debra Fileta**, M.A., LPC National Speaker and Bestselling Author of *Reset*

No relationship will contribute more to your satisfaction (or dissatisfaction) in life than marriage. And the starting point of every marriage is dating: Dating lays the foundation upon which marriages are built. So I'm so glad to see a book addressing this important subject and giving us practical tips on how to approach this critical phase in a godly manner—all based on the timeless wisdom of our ancient Church Fathers.

—**Fr. Anthony Messeh**, author of *Whatever, God*

To my husband, Fr. Antony Andrews:
thank you for being the patient,
loving, and God-fearing man
who I'm blessed to be with on this journey.

To my little girls, Amelia, Hannah, and Rebecca,
who I pray one day will become godly women:
may your lives be encompassed by
endless grace and fruitfulness.

Contents

Part 2: The Dating

INTRODUCTION

When I was a little girl, maybe five or six years old, my family took a vacation I had been anticipating for a long time. We stayed in a beach house a few yards away from one of Egypt's Red Sea shores. As my family unpacked and settled in, I changed into my swimsuit and raced to the edge of the water. The waves were enticing for a little girl who wanted nothing more than to plunge into the water, but I was only a few feet tall and hadn't yet learned to swim. Still, I rushed into the glistening sea, only to be greeted by brutal waves. Within a matter of seconds, I found myself tumbling down, unable to take a breath or get my bearings. Miraculously, my older cousin saw me and snatched me out of the water. The event certainly scared my parents; I'm sure they reprimanded me afterward. Even though I was more careful the rest of the vacation, I still thought about when I could jump in again.

I have always loved the beach: how the waves bring endless freshness on a hot summer day, the heat leaves my skin warm and sun-kissed, and my feet magically sink into the sand and disappear. Romantic life can feel similar: brimming with warm feelings that leave our hearts full and our faces beaming with joy. But unfortunately, we sometimes do what I did on my first day on the beach with our romantic life; we jump in too early without being ready. The world's depictions of dating are so captivating that we sometimes forget how it can make our hearts weary if we approach it without a plan. When we date at the wrong time or without an accurate understanding of the process, we struggle to stay afloat, not knowing how to escape its currents.

Just as the ocean's cool water is reenergizing on a hot summer day for a swimmer, getting to know someone and seeing how delicately God made them can feel electrifying in a relationship. And being intimate with someone in the context of marriage can be a glorious, bonding experience. But water is not only life-giving but also powerful, sometimes even causing injury. Similarly, dating can be confusing and disheartening, and it can even leave us with a soul-crushing injury, causing us to never want to experience it again. And if we date the way secular culture tells us to, there's a great chance we'll follow our instincts and let ourselves be lured by lust, chasing after sexual temptations. By doing so, we welcome sin into our dating relationships, which will lead us down the wrong path and deter us from the right approach to dating.

Additionally, when we enter marriage with unhealthy expectations it can leave us miserable and lonely. If we are unaware of the salvific purpose of marriage, we might chase it for the wrong reasons, and if we only look for earthly happiness, we'll be disappointed whenever our spouse doesn't meet our expectations. We need to keep in mind that the fundamental goal of marriage is holiness, not temporary happiness.

Nonetheless, God made marriage beautiful, the ultimate gift of companionship—and we see this throughout Scripture. God gave Sarah to Abraham, to accompany him on his adventures of faith (Gen. 11:29). He didn't let Ruth stay a widow but brought her to Boaz (Ruth 4:13). He paired Priscilla and Aquila, knowing they would be an instrumental couple as missionaries in the early Church (Acts 18:2). Indeed, lack of companionship was the only thing God deemed "not good" within all the goodness of creation: "And the LORD God said, '*It is* not good that man should be alone; I will make him a helper comparable to him'" (Gen. 2:18).

Today, we must navigate the impoverished ideas of dating found in popular culture, which are often self-serving. Some date to escape loneliness, aimlessly jumping from one relationship to another. Some date because it's the popular thing to do, and it seems fun. Others date because they truly desire companionship. As Orthodox Christians, we should date to get to know someone to discover if they would be a suitable long-term partner and the right choice for a spouse. The companionship we seek shouldn't just be temporary but the starting path to a lifelong partnership. We aim for the final destination, where two become one and practice selflessness and sacrifice. So before embarking on the dating journey, we want to be ready and know what to look for in a partner. During the dating process we want to discover more about our partner and evaluate compatibility. Gathering all the necessary facts along the way will help us make one of the biggest decisions in life: whom to marry.

In contrast to secular ideas about dating, purity culture and some church communities can foster a negative perception of dating— perhaps as a reaction against painful experiences or hollow versions of dating found in the secular world. Indeed, purity culture even encouraged Christians not to date at all in order to avoid the sexual temptation of premarital sex (we'll get more into this in chapter 3). While it is important to follow God's commandments and save sex for marriage, it is equally important to understand His design for marriage and sex. Seeing the big picture, instead of eliminating dating altogether, is imperative for moving in the right direction.

Despite these warring factions in our culture, it is still possible, even healthy, to learn and practice a balanced approach to dating. This is good news. We don't have to frown upon it. And our dating journey doesn't have to be a walk in the dark; it can be a path that helps us flourish. There's a way to get to know someone for the purpose of possibly getting married, while also honoring God, ourselves, and each other. And there's a productive way to be in periods of singleness as well. That's what I offer in this book— ways to navigate the dating seasons in life as well as the seasons of singleness. Sometimes they're intertwined, when we may oscillate between them; at other times, they're distinctly separated by longer periods of singleness.

I pray this book will help many readers navigate the tricky terrain of dating, purity, sex, and singleness. But first, let's get to know each other a bit.

The Author

I've been a wife for a decade and a priest's wife for seven of those years. I'm also a mom of three girls, an engineer, a certified life coach, a blogger, a speaker, and now an author. I'm passionate about youth ministry and have been involved in it for the last fifteen years in the Coptic Orthodox Church. I am also someone who loves God and is perpetually trying to deepen my connection with Him. I am so in awe of God's love that I want others to experience it too. In these pages, I hope to spread a godly message about dating and singleness to this generation and the generations to come.

Born in Egypt, a country about 6,000 miles away from where I live now, I spent much of my youth merging two different worldviews to form my identity. Transitioning from one country to another at eight years old was not a smooth operation. I had to learn a new language while keeping my first language alive. I had to understand new customs, traditions, and social norms and find a way for them to exist with my current beliefs. Both cultures have many valuable things to offer, but both have imperfections. I am someone who loves her church and its deep roots, but I am also fond of the helpful lessons I've learned from Western culture.

I spent the majority of my teenage years trying not to date before I was ready, and trying to control my sexual desires and not fall into the peer pressure of having a boyfriend. Sometimes I fell short, and other times I succeeded by the grace of God. I'm here to tell you that no matter how hard dating in a godly manner may feel, there is a light at the end of the tunnel. God is always there to strengthen you as you seek to obey His commandments for purity and holiness, "For this is the will of God, your sanctification" (1 Thess. 4:3).

I pray that your heart and mind will be open to the message of this book and, ultimately, to whatever God has for you in particular. I hope the book serves as a tool to point you to the most perfect book of all time, the Bible, where you can truly hear God's voice. My prayer for this book is for God to miraculously bless it as He blessed the feeding of the five thousand (Matt. 14:13–21). That story has always been one of my favorite miracles, and my family has an icon of it hung above our dining table to remind us that God will always bless the little we have to offer. That's what I hope this book is: a small offering being given to God to bless and transform into abundant nourishment for whoever reads the pages that follow. A book that will feed its readers and not leave them spiritually hungry. And one that communicates the message through speaking the truth in love (which I discovered is not an easy balance to master).

· · · · ·

While interacting with young adults through my church ministry, I saw the struggles they were facing when it came to dating. My passion for helping them navigate these critical times led me to pursue a life coaching certification through the International Coaching Federation (ICF).

Coaching allows a client to find clarity in an area that feels foggy to them. It eliminates the haze and helps them identify a direct path to their goal. Coaching acts as the catalyst they need to change their life for the better. Unlike therapy, which helps a client understand their past or work on mental health issues, coaching is all about moving forward without diving too deep into the past (many coaching clients also work with a therapist at the same time, for different purposes). Using coaching methods, I am able to help various single, dating, and engaged clients make the improvements they needed to transform their romantic lives. I have filled these pages with similar techniques and exercises in hopes of equipping you to do the same: to set and reach your relationship goals.

Book Road Map

Initially, I intended this book to focus only on the dating phase, not the struggles that precede it in the waiting stage. Not only is there enough to say about dating to fill an entire book, but I also enjoy writing about it. But too many marriages begin and end because the couple skipped over some fundamental steps before or during dating, and skipping these steps can ultimately lead to pain and heartbreak. A right understanding of marriage will help you pick a partner that has the qualities needed for a successful marriage. And getting to know that person while dating to determine if they are the right partner will increase the likelihood that your marriage will thrive. Studies have found that couples who dated longer are less likely to get divorced; one concluded that couples who date for one or two years were 20 percent less likely to divorce compared to those who dated for a shorter amount of time.[1]

* * * * *

Part 1 of this book identifies two paths that lead to salvation—singleness and marriage—and focuses on singleness. Some willingly choose a life of celibacy and ministry. Others are single for long periods due to circumstances beyond their control, and some are single for a short time before beginning to date. These latter two stages will be the main ones addressed in part 1.

Part 1 also explores how your view of dating starts with ideas and expectations you conjure up while single, and how your readiness for dating plays a critical role in the success of your relationships. If you start dating prematurely, you might find yourself in a toxic relationship and not be able to recognize the dangers of it. Studies have found that toxic dating relationships can affect the mental and physical health of teenagers, exposing them to problems such as drug use, violence, and abuse. And because teenage brains are still developing, signs of toxicity in relationships may go undetected.[2] While this may sound scary, there's much you can learn and practice while you are single to put you on a path for a future healthy and fruitful romantic relationship. For this reason, this book includes thoughts and strategies for singleness and seasons of waiting. If you

---

1   Andrew Francis-Tan and Hugo M. Mialon, "'A Diamond Is Forever' and Other Fairy Tales: The Relationship between Wedding Expenses and Marriage Duration," *Economic Inquiry* 53, no. 4 (March 10, 2015): https://onlinelibrary.wiley.com/doi/abs/10.1111/ecin.12206.

2   "Troubled Teenage Relationships Can Have Lasting Health Consequences," NBC News, May 1, 2023, https://www.nbcnews.com/health/health-news/troubled-teen-relationships-can-lasting-health-problems-research-finds-rcna81562.

understand and implement many of the pre-dating concepts discussed, you will have an easier time figuring out how to date.

Part 2 jumps into the dating phase and the healthy mentalities and boundaries that will help you with it. Dating is about getting to know someone with the ultimate goal of pursuing marriage if they are a suitable fit. This doesn't necessarily mean marrying the person you're dating; rather, it means deciding if they are the right partner for you. Knowing *what* you are looking for is essential before you can find *who* you are looking for. Compatibility also plays a significant part in the success of a relationship. A couple's compatibility is discussed in detail, and what to do when it is lacking.

In the last section, Part 3, I share key tools for honoring God during the waiting and dating phases. Topics like purity, sexuality, temptations, and repentance are defined and examined under the light of Scripture and the ancient wisdom of the Church Fathers. Each chapter offers hope to any state we might find ourselves in and a plan for staying on, or returning to, the godly path we are all called to.

At the end of every chapter, I share popular beliefs that are actually myths, to challenge you to reconsider some common misconceptions you might have heard about each topic. Digging through the lies you've accumulated to find the truth that will set you free is crucial. Each myth invites you to question your mistaken beliefs and distinguish the lies from the truth.

· · · · ·

This book is for virtually any older teenager, as well as dating or single-but-looking young adults, regardless of background. If you are a teenager trying to figure out what to do with all your romantic feelings and wondering whether dating is right for you, this book is for you. This book will also be helpful if you are a young adult, ready to date and meet the love of your life, and you want to know how to do it well. Additionally, you'll find value in the book if you are trying to make peace with the state of singleness you find yourself currently in.

If you are trying to honor God and resist the temptations of a sexually saturated world, this book will guide you. And if you need help to unlearn harmful ideas about sex and sexuality you might have grown up with (or are currently growing up with), this book will help you with precisely that. If you are trying to live a pure life again and regretting mistakes you have made in the past, you might particularly enjoy the last chapter of the book.

·   ·   ·   ·   ·

How young is too young to start reading about dating? If you're a parent, even if your teen is not yet ready to date, it's never too early to introduce them to healthy forms of preparation so they can understand the process. Developing a clear picture of the final destination can help teens and young people gauge whether they are ready and on the right path to begin dating. It's also never too early to understand God's intention and design for sex, so it can be honored and revered along the way as it ought to be. It's also useful for parents and ministry leaders to be reminded of these things and to explore whether their own understandings and teachings about singleness, dating, purity, and sexuality remain consistent with Christian values.

Getting ready to date doesn't start with preparing for a first date and trying to push the butterflies aside. It begins with educating yourself about healthy dating and about how healthy waiting is the key to getting there. It's also about recognizing when that time is right. Jumping in at the wrong time and without the proper foundation can leave you tumbling in the tumultuous waves of complex relationships. So, fasten your life jackets and get ready to learn how to swim in and navigate the brisk but beautiful waters of waiting and dating.

Note: In the real-life stories you'll find in this book, all names have been changed to protect the privacy of the people who appear in them.

PART 1

The Waiting

1

Stay Single or Mingle?

When I was in college, I met a handsome young man. Mutual friends introduced us. I don't remember our first conversation, but I remember the impression he left on me. He had a certain demeanor about him. He was calm, collected, observant, and of very few words—a true introvert. There were some signs that he was thinking about the monastic path. He would spend his winter and summer breaks in Coptic Orthodox monasteries in the US and Egypt. You could always find him reading or discussing a spiritual book, mainly ones highlighting the lives and wisdom of the Desert Fathers. He immersed himself in the liturgical life of the Church and made some appearances in social gatherings.

We would sit with a small group of friends and share what we'd been reading, what ministries we were involved in, and how our different parishes ran things. Once in a while, we would read the Bible together and have an impromptu Bible study. I watched how everyone respected him and sought guidance from him.

Throughout his college years, he struggled to discern whether to pursue a life of celibacy or marriage. Two very different paths were tugging on his heart, pulling him in opposite directions. He was seeking God's will for his life and trying to figure out his calling—a calling to flee the world or stay in it. With the help of those guiding him (his circle of guidance) and with many prayers, he was eventually able to make the right decision for himself.

This young man later became Fr. Antony, my husband. In hindsight, his pursuit of the monastic path was a blessing in disguise; it made me put him in the "friend" category (i.e., the friend zone) rather than the "potential spouse" category, which contributed to forming a healthy, God-fearing platonic friendship, which I enjoyed greatly.

How many of us first stop to discern God's will for our marital life before picking a path for ourselves? What if God wants us to marry, and we want to remain single? Or what if He wants us to devote our entire life to only serving Him, but we want to get married? Whichever path He guides us toward, the end goal is the same—the Kingdom.

Two Paths to Salvation: Marriage and Singleness

Salvation is the ultimate goal of every Christian's life, and by the grace of God we can reach that goal by taking the path of singleness or of marriage. Take a look at St. Paul and St. Peter for example, two influential apostles who boldly professed the Good News, stood fearlessly in the face of threats, and laid down their lives for the Kingdom. Saint Peter was married, and St. Paul was celibate (although the Bible doesn't mention his marital status, we know from his letters to the Corinthians he was celibate at the time of writing them). Both brought glory to God through their ministries and gained the Kingdom.

Father Josiah Trenham, in his book *On Marriage and Virginity According to St. John Chrysostom*, talks further about how celibacy works in a similar way to marriage as we pursue the path of salvation:

> Virginity works as should truly Christian marriage, to accomplish the divine task of reducing the baseness of our souls and leading them to perfect virtue. God has called us to one ambition only: to regain Paradise lost. Success in the battle against the devil and victory over evil is the path of return, and constitutes the reacquisition of the virginal life of Paradise. Whether one travels there by virginity, which is the most direct route, or by the blessed state of earthly marriage is not God's main concern; it is the return to Paradise itself that is important.[3]

Both life paths help refine, sanctify, and bring us closer to God to attain salvation. Even if one initially sets out on a life that avoids both celibacy *and* marriage, pursuing their desires without any commitments, there is still a way to reroute and seek union with God. Deciding to flee sexual immorality (1 Cor. 6:18), instead of continuing to run toward it, is another way to regain that Paradise lost. The question is, which path will you take to return to Paradise?

• • • • •

From the beginning of creation, God created Adam and did not want him to be alone—so He created for him a helpmate comparable to him. The foundational biblical stories of our faith highlight many God-fearing marriages. In addition to the marriages I mentioned in the introduction to this book, we also see Adam and

---

3   Archpriest Josiah B. Trenham, *Marriage and Virginity According to St. John Chrysostom* (Platina, CA: St. Herman of Alaska Brotherhood, 2013), 114.

Eve (Gen. 2:21–25), Isaac and Rebekah (Gen. 24), Moses and Zipporah (Ex. 2:21), Elkanah and Hannah (1 Sam. 1:1–2), and Zacharias and Elizabeth (Luke 1:5), to name a few.

Scripture and the Church Fathers agreed that there were three main reasons for marriage: the first was for procreation. The Jewish way of life in the Old Testament stressed the necessity of marriage in terms of procreation. In fact, if you couldn't get married and bear children, not only was this frowned upon, but some believed God was punishing you for a sin you had committed. Getting married was the way the human race was built and preserved, and procreation was seen as the ultimate goal and duty of every law-abiding Jew. The only exceptions were if God asked you to be celibate (like He did in Jer. 16:1–2) or if you were a eunuch. Saint John Chrysostom states that besides chastity, the reason marriage was instituted was to make us parents.[4] He also believes that children are a kind of bridge that join together the flesh of the mother and father.[5]

In addition to procreation, the second way Scripture and the Church Fathers saw marriage was as a means to flee sexual immorality. For example, St. Paul starts 1 Corinthians 7 by speaking about this. Although it is not the only reason for marriage, it was a solution to the temptations the Corinthians were facing. It is important to understand that he was addressing the people in Corinth who lived a carnal life full of wickedness and sexual immorality (1 Cor. 5:1), and for the sake of their purity he suggests a holy matrimony in which a wife and husband ought to give themselves to one another (see 1 Cor. 7:1–5). Saint John Chrysostom also addresses the issue,

---

4   John Chrysostom, *On Marriage and Family Life,* trans. Catharine P. Roth and David Anderson (Yonkers, NY: St Vladimir's Seminary Press, 1986), 85.
5   Chrysostom, 20.

saying, "Marriage was created as a harbor in the storm and to prevent unlawful unions. While married persons have this harbor, the virgin 'sails a harborless ocean.'"[6]

Finally, Scripture and the Church Fathers also saw marriage as important because of the marital bond. Saint Augustine, a prominent Christian theologian, writes, "In matrimony, however, let these nuptial blessings be the objects of our love—offspring, fidelity, the sacramental bond."[7] When St. Augustine discussed the concept of the nuptial bond in the context of marriage, he emphasized the spiritual dimension of the marital union, viewing it as a reflection of the relationship between Christ and the Church. He believed that the love and unity between husband and wife mirrored the unity between Christ and believers, as it is addressed in Ephesians 5:22–26:

> Wives, submit to your own husbands, as to the Lord. For the husband is head of the wife, as also Christ is head of the church; and He is the Savior of the body. Therefore, just as the church is subject to Christ, so *let* the wives *be* to their own husbands in everything. Husbands, love your wives, just as Christ also loved the church and gave Himself for her, that He might sanctify and cleanse her with the washing of water by the word.

This perspective influenced Christian theology on marriage, highlighting its sacred and symbolic significance.

---

6 Trenham, *Marriage and Virginity*, 102.
7 Augustine, *On Marriage and Concupiscence*, bk. I, ch.19, New Advent, accessed July 15, 2022, https://www.newadvent.org/fathers/15071.htm.

· · · · ·

On the other hand, many of our Orthodox pillars, such as our Church Fathers and our Desert Fathers and Mothers, lived a life of celibacy and were fully committed to the Lord—not to mention that Christ was also single yet became the bridegroom of the Church. When St. Paul writes, "But I want you to be without care. He who is unmarried cares for the things of the Lord—how he may please the Lord" (1 Cor. 7:32), he reminds us that it is honorable to want to devote our life to God and focus only on pleasing Him. So some desire a life of singleness; how they live out that desire can take a few different forms. They may want a life of solitude and to spend all their days focused on worshiping the Lord in a monastery or convent and live in a community that seeks the same priorities. Some might want to remain in society and serve God wholeheartedly without the responsibility of a spouse or children; therefore, they will choose to stay single but consecrate themselves to carrying out the work of God in the world.

Others might try dating while they work to decipher God's will and later realize they were meant for a life of singleness and complete devotion to Christ. Or some might desire marriage but never find the opportunity; they may set out to find a suitable spouse but struggle to do so. Then, after years of trying to find a compatible partner, they may accept that their current state of singleness and celibacy is no longer temporary. Still, it's the path that will lead to their salvation. It might take a person some time—and even mourning—to accept the calling of singleness God has directed them toward. Saying goodbye to a life they thought they would have is not easy, but grieving that vision is essential in order to be able to move forward. It might take a long time, or even a lifetime, to make peace with their singleness, but embracing their newfound destination will help them transform their goals and dreams to better fit their life.

It's important to keep in mind that neither married couples nor celibate people are greater than the other: both are on different paths to holiness that draw them closer to God. Although some might view celibacy as the holier path, St. John Chrysostom tells us to "remind one another that nothing in life is to be feared, except offending God. If your marriage is like this, your perfection will rival the holiest of monks."[8] Also, it's paramount to remember that there is no linear definition of a successful life. Success looks different for each individual, but the one universal objective of every Christian soul is salvation—an endeavor that all can agree on, married or single.

The critical thing we all must discern is which path is for us. But even if we feel perplexed and can't discern the right path, God will bless our faithfulness. And even if we misinterpret the correct answer, when we submit to God's will, He will direct or redirect us to the right path. If you walk with the Lord and build a relationship with Him where you can decipher His voice, it will help you discern what He is calling you to. Try looking at how He has answered your previous prayers. How does He typically talk to you? For me, God has always clearly shut the doors on opportunities I wasn't supposed to take and opened doors for where He wanted me to go. But this is different for everyone; you must figure out what it looks like in your life.

Mother Teresa, at the young age of twelve, heard God call her to the religious life.[9] Setting out to become a religious sister at the age of eighteen, she spent years in ministry before she heard another call. In 1946 while visiting the slums of Calcutta, India, she felt God calling her to do more work among the poor there. After spending

---

8   Chrysostom, *On Marriage & Family Life*, 61.
9   Kathryn Spink, *Mother Teresa: A Complete Authorized Biography* (New York: HarperCollins, 1998), 23–43.

time in deep prayer and retreat, she knew this was her "call within a call." Just like Mother Teresa, when God places certain desires on our heart to serve Him, we must immerse ourselves in prayer to be able to decipher His call.

Submitting to God's Will

As we have seen, discerning God's call can be difficult, as can submitting to His will. So let me share with you how one couple did it: Ephraim and Ava. Ephraim was raised in a devout Orthodox Christian home. He became closer to God and his Orthodox community during his college years through campus ministries and his local parish. He developed a deep love for service, and God blessed him with many talents to carry out his ministries.

Ever since he could remember, he had desired marriage and fatherhood and kept praying that God would fulfill that desire, and during his college and young adult years, he met many incredible Orthodox Christian women and had a few serious relationships, but none that led to marriage. After breaking up with a woman he thought he would marry, Ephraim was disappointed and dejected. He began to question whether God intended marriage for him, and if He did, why He was making it so hard for him to find the right person. Ephraim became frustrated with dating and took a break for a few years. During those years, he focused on building his relationship with God and immersed himself in youth ministries, which led to personal and spiritual growth. He still desired marriage and was open to meeting new people.

When Ephraim was entering his late thirties, his father confessor (or "father of confession" as referred to in the Coptic tradition) challenged him to submit to God's will, even if God's will for him was celibacy (not monasticism, but celibacy in the world). That wasn't what he wanted to hear, since he had longed for companionship his entire adult life. But he began to wrestle with the idea anyway, and he slowly made his peace with it.

One day he was attending a midweek liturgy at his parish during Lent and noticed a woman standing next to a lovely elderly couple he knew, but he couldn't tell who she was, because of her head covering and Covid mask. At this point, he was in his early forties and thought he already knew everyone who attended his parish. After the liturgy ended, he approached the couple and realized it was their daughter, Ava, a woman in her late thirties.

Ava had grown up in the same large parish as Ephraim, and while he was serving inside the parish, she was serving outside of it. She had spent a few years doing missionary work in South America and had lived in different states over the years due to her medical studies and training. Since their parish was large, with hundreds of families, they never got a chance to get to know each other.

Ava also grew up in a devout Orthodox Christian home with a slightly different ethnic background than Ephraim. She was a beautiful woman, inside and out, and she had tried dating various men over the years, but they either didn't have the God-fearing relationship she was looking for or they weren't compatible with her. Ava also desired marriage and motherhood, but after spending years longing for it, with dating relationships not working out, she began to question if marriage was her path. Ava tried deciphering God's will and accepted that singleness was her calling. She fully embraced it and spent time in missionary services in Bolivia until God called her back to the US. She then dedicated her life to serving others as a physician and gladly endured the hard trials of the COVID-19 pandemic as a first responder.

Ephraim and Ava were walking on separate paths with God, fully trusting in His plan. They never doubted His goodness and faithfulness but had to make their peace with what could have been a lifelong calling for singleness. Through all of it, they focused on the One who mattered the most. It wasn't only in their outward church attendance or public ministries that they found God but in their hidden rooms, in prayer, trials, tribulations, and victories. God had used every hardship in their lives to shape them, and they chose to let those hardships bring them closer to God instead of drawing them further from Him. And when it was the fullness of time—the right time for them—God brought them together, not because they were chasing each other but because they were chasing Him. They are now happily married and expecting their first child.

· · · · ·

As we see from the example of Ava and Ephraim, sometimes God's timeline and plan will look very different from ours. As teens we might be eager to start dating as soon as possible, and as young adults we may be yearning to start married life, but God might be moving at a different pace, and we will need to find a way to accept that.

We may also need to give up on our own desires and instead search for what God desires for us. Instead of insisting that we must be married, we ought to be open to God's plan, even if it differs from ours—for God knows the true, godly desires of our hearts, and He works with us to fulfill them out of His goodness and love for us. Psalm 37:4 is a popular verse often used to highlight God's promise to fulfill our desires: "Delight yourself also in the LORD, / And He shall give you the desires of your heart," but people often overlook the first half of the verse: delighting ourselves in the Lord. When we delight in the Lord, we become wrapped up in Him and His love. Then our desires will begin to reflect His heart—which turns our desires, whether they may be selfish, shallow, or even good, into godly desires. And our godly desires will get us closer to Him; they will be pure and bear the fruit of the Spirit (even the fruit of long-suffering). So then, if our desires are godly, God would undoubtedly grant them because they will lead us to Him.

Giving up on our desires and being open to God's can be a struggle, not just in singleness but during every stage in our life. There are a few things you can focus on in your season of singleness that will bring you closer to fulfilling your godly desires, such as growing in patience, enjoying the benefits of that season, and building a circle of people who can guide you.

Growing in Patience

When we set out to gain a spiritual virtue, we sometimes imagine the end result and overlook the hard work it takes to get there. For example, patience is a spiritual virtue we often pray for, yet we might not willingly endure the suffering it takes to gain it. Instead, we want God to automatically make us patient, like how He blessed King Solomon with wisdom upon his request (1 Kin. 3). Living in today's fast-paced world, we tend to equate waiting with inefficiency, and we think that if we were smart enough, we would find ways to shorten waiting periods or eliminate them altogether. But patience often results from walking through uncomfortable, sometimes excruciating, trials and continuing to wait on God.

Throughout the Bible, we witness the blessings of remaining patient through trials of waiting. Moses waited forty years in Midian tending sheep before God called him to be a bold and faithful leader (Acts 7:29–30). Abraham and Sarah waited twenty-five years for a son from the time God promised them a child (Gen. 21:1–5). Jacob waited fourteen years to marry Rachel after being deceived into marrying her sister Leah after the first seven years of working for their father (Gen. 29:20–28). David waited over a decade to become king from the time Samuel anointed him as God's chosen (1 Sam. 16:13; 2 Sam. 5:4). And in all their waiting, God was refining and preparing them for the greater things to come.

Moses grew in humility when he ran away from living a prestigious life in Pharaoh's house to tend sheep in the wilderness, so that when God asked him to go back to Egypt and lead the Israelites to the Promised Land, he led in meekness (Num. 12:3). Abraham grew in faith waiting for Isaac all those years, so that when God tested Him by asking him to sacrifice his only son, he willingly obliged (Gen. 22:1–19). Jacob gained endurance working for his father-in-law for fourteen years for Rachel's hand in marriage, and when he wrestled with God, he wouldn't give up until he had received His blessing (Gen. 32:24–28). David spent years running from Saul, learning to make God his refuge, and became a man after God's own heart (Acts 13:22).

Waiting often produces virtuous fruit that would not be gained otherwise, as Fr. Kyrillos Ibrahim tells us when he meditates on the words of the Psalmist, "How long, O Lord? Will You forget me forever? / How long will You hide Your face from me?" (Ps. 13:1). He writes, "Waiting, therefore, is an essential element in the spiritual life. But it is not an empty waiting, because we know that God is present and fills every moment. The key is to let God give meaning to our waiting and not insist on our own expectations of how our waiting should be fulfilled."[10]

So if marriage is in God's plan for us, then remaining patient during the period of singleness will make this time fruitful, not idle, because singleness can be full of trials that yield the virtues required

---

10   Fr. Kyrillos Ibrahim, *All That I Have Is Yours: 100 Meditations with St. Pope Kyrillos VI on the Spiritual Life* (Anaheim, CA: ACTS Press, 2021), 23.

for a strong marriage. For example, learning to serve God fully while single will help you serve your spouse in marriage. Enduring periods of loneliness while single will build independence and reliance on God, which you will also need in marriage. Praying for God to fulfill the desires of your heart while single will give you the stamina to pray during spiritual battles that you will endure in marriage. And struggles you fight through in singleness will become sources of your strength when you are married.

Even if singleness does not end up being a part of waiting for marriage for you but becomes a permanent state, it will still be part of waiting for the Kingdom. Serving God in abundance will allow you to grow closer to Him and prepare you to spend eternity with Him. Battling the feeling of loneliness will allow you to lean on Him for the comfort no human can provide. And praying unceasingly will strengthen your communication with Him, making Him the One you rely on.

My friend Macrina is a great example of how struggling and learning patience in the waiting can produce fruit in your life. She is a devout Orthodox Christian who strives to grow in her faith. During her teenage and young adult years, she envisioned that she would settle down with a husband and start growing her family in her twenties, but her path to marriage has been bumpy. She is now a successful professional in her midthirties and has been in and out of relationships, searching for the right person. She's dated great Christian men, yet every relationship ended due to a lack of compatibility.

I spoke to Macrina during her season of singleness and asked her a bold question: "How do you know God is not calling you to a lifetime of singleness?" She admitted that this was an idea she often battled with. When she spoke to her father confessor about her struggle, she said to him, "Maybe God doesn't want me to get married. Maybe He wants me to stay single." But she knew in her heart that she was only saying this to suppress the pain she felt about being single. Her father confessor wisely answered, "If it's God's will for you to be single, you wouldn't feel like you're settling; you'd feel peace about setting out on this path." She doesn't feel that peace yet, so she continues to pray until God gives her peace around being single or until He sends her the right spouse.

Macrina remains patient and trusts that her heavenly Father, who is a giver of good gifts, will answer her desire, for in Matthew 7:11 Christ says, "If you then, being evil, know how to give good gifts to your children, how much more will your Father who is in heaven give good things to those who ask Him!" So until He fulfills her desire for marriage or her desire is fulfilled in another way, she'll keep praying for His will while having hope in His promise. When someone asks her if she's married, she replies, "No, not yet." Her current singleness has sharpened her and taught her to rely on God for all things. The fruit of her waiting has resulted in a stronger relationship with God and she has grown in patience because of the experience.

In every big life decision, Macrina took the same steps we all should strive to take. She prayed for God's will and she sought the guidance of those who know her well. She would always wait patiently to feel at peace before making any significant decision— the kind of peace that surpasses all understanding, as St. Paul writes, "Be anxious for nothing, but in everything by prayer and supplication, with thanksgiving, let your requests be made known to God; and the peace of God, which surpasses all understanding, will guard your hearts and minds through Christ Jesus" (Phil. 4:6– 7). This peace is easier for some to feel than others, and it might be harder to discern for those who struggle with anxiety and depression or other mental health issues. But Macrina was able to figure out how to sense that peace as she developed her relationship with God. Her season of singleness has borne many fruits thus far.

Enjoying the Benefits of Singleness

How many days and nights do we spend daydreaming, hoping, and praying that we will find the right person? How much effort goes into chasing after our crushes? How many moments do we waste just waiting around to be in a relationship? If I answered those questions honestly, my responses would make you cringe. I spent countless moments doing all those things instead of enjoying my singleness. I saw my single days as lonely, sad days instead of finding purpose in them.

You might have heard the famous Christian saying that "singleness is a gift." But some of you may be looking for the receipt to return this so-called gift. You feel like your life will fully start only once you're locked in the arms of a significant other. But your life has already begun, so it's best to strive to live in the now, rather than in the future. You can live a deeply fulfilling life enriched with adventures and thrilling experiences, quiet moments that lead to aha moments, spiritual and emotional growth, friendships that bring out the very best in you, and journeys that take you deep in and bring you back stronger, smarter, and wiser than you ever were.

Saint Paul highlights some of the great benefits of staying unmarried when he writes the following:

But I want you to be without care. He who is unmarried cares for the things of the Lord—how he may please the Lord. But he who is married *cares* about the things of the world—how he may please *his* wife . . . The unmarried woman cares about the things of the Lord, that she may be holy both in body and in spirit. But she who is married cares about the things of the world—how she may please *her* husband. (1 Cor. 7:32–34)

In these verses St. Paul shows how being unmarried allows one to concentrate on worshipping and serving God, whereas one who is married would be distracted by the cares and concerns that come with having a spouse. Nourishing and attending to your marriage requires much effort, and sometimes creates stress and anxiety. The ESV translation of verse 32 reads, "I want you to be free from anxieties." Free from anxiety? That sounds like a gift to me!

Being single also gives you the gift of time that many married people and parents would love to have a little more of; indeed, if you get married and/or have children in the future, you may find yourself at times looking back wistfully on your days of singlehood. While you are single, you have the freedom to figure out what you want to devote your time and energy to. You can do many things without worrying about the time you'd have to give someone else if you were in a relationship. And you can freely invest in yourself and focus on your education and career while spending your money as you see fit.

You can also choose to dedicate more time to God in various ways: For example, you have the freedom to show up to any church service you choose and to participate in the life of your parish in any way and as much as you would like. Or you could go on any mission trips and spiritual conferences that interest you. Some of my most formative experiences occurred during mission trips to Africa I took during my college years, as well as during the days I spent on spiritual retreats in monasteries and convents. I didn't have to worry about splitting the limited number of days off I could take from work between vacationing with my family and taking a spiritual trip. I didn't have to figure out babysitting plans if I wanted to volunteer for a ministry. I didn't have to worry about caring for crying babies during Liturgy and wrestling to utter a few uninterrupted prayers. I wasn't distracted by screaming toddlers as I delivered the message in a youth meeting. These are all real examples from my current life, and while I adore serving my kids (and motherhood is also a ministry), it comes with its own challenges.

When you're young and free, you can also build a beautiful relationship with the Lord without many interruptions, and those moments you spend with Him will sustain you when busier and sometimes more challenging times come, as Ecclesiastes 12:1 says, "Remember now your Creator in the days of your youth, / Before the difficult days come."

Singleness is also a great time to enjoy and invest in valuable relationships with friends, mentors, and family. Taking time to grow and strengthen your relationships with friends and mentors will be of great value as you travel into different seasons of life. These relationships will provide valuable lifelines during busy and/or difficult times, and no matter how wonderful a connection you have with your spouse, your spouse cannot and should not fulfill all your relational needs. While you are single, you can easily spend time with your family members since you don't have to divide your time between them and your partner's family. These might even turn out to be precious days you get with your aging parents or older family members that you will never have again. And spending time with your elders and learning from them is also vital to building your circle of guidance.

Build Your Circle of Guidance

When I was younger, I had my whole life meticulously planned out. I played out every scene when it came to settling down and getting married, and it made perfect sense in my head. I would graduate college with my bachelor's degree in civil engineering, find the ideal job, climb up the corporate ladder, make enough money to spend on myself, travel to see the world, and get a master's degree that my great job would pay for. Then, when I had "lived" a little, I'd finally settle down. I hoped to meet the right person by my mid to late twenties, spend a few years enjoying married life, and start having kids by age thirty.

These plans make me laugh now! Instead of following my perfect plan, I met my husband when I started college, we started dating three years later, and we got married soon after graduating. And by the time I hit thirty, I had already given birth to three beautiful little girls. When my husband first asked me out, he caught me by surprise, but in the best possible way. As I shared earlier, I thought marriage wasn't in his plans. But when he expressed his interest in a relationship, I was giddy at the possibility of being with him. We had spent three years in college being good friends and bonding over our mutual love for books, service, and spirituality. I knew his character and was attracted to him. But his timing didn't exactly fit into my ten-year plan.

There was another hurdle we'd have to get through to start our relationship off on the right foot: getting our parents' blessing to date. Unless you are part of an ethnic Orthodox community with strict views around dating (like in my case), most parents of young adults don't require them to ask for permission to date. But if you're in your teen years, or just coming out of them, you might want to get your parents on board with the idea of you dating. And regardless of your age, it's good for you and your parents to be on the same page, as they will have an important role in guiding your choices that lead to marriage.

My future husband's parents were excited to hear that he was second-guessing his choice about entering into the monastic life: they could have more time with him and possibly have grandchildren, if he didn't. It brought his mom to tears (of joy), and he got an immediate green light from them. My parents, on the other hand, were reluctant at first but after a few conversations about what dating would be like for us they were on board.

* * * * *

As this story from my life demonstrates, whenever you're facing a big decision—whether you're discerning your marital path, a career, a big move, or something else—you should have a circle of trusted people you reach out to for guidance. I'll refer to this as your "circle of guidance" throughout the rest of the book. Your circle of guidance should consist of family, a spiritual father, and mentors, all of whom are God-fearing people who always have your best interests at heart.

Diagram 1: Circle of Guidance

If your parents don't fulfill the family role or are not around, you might have other parental figures you can trust. Family guidance can also come from older siblings, aunts, uncles, grandparents, cousins, or anyone who knows you well, demonstrates wisdom, and honors God.

A spiritual father can be your father confessor or another priest you regularly go to for spiritual direction. You should have invested time in building a relationship with him so that he knows you well enough to know your strengths and weaknesses and can guide you accordingly.

Mentors are people you admire and look up to.[11] They are typically at least ten years older than you and can be older friends, church ministry leaders, teachers, or coaches. Mentoring works best if this person is someone who has walked through what you're currently trying to navigate and has done it while honoring God. For example, if you're seeking relationship advice, look for someone who has a successful marriage, one that is striving toward holiness.

The role of your circle of guidance is not to tell you what to do but to help you gain clarity around big and small life decisions. With their help, it will be easier to make the right decision. Building trust with each person in your circle of guidance takes time and vulnerability, and you must be willing to open up to them and share your thoughts and feelings without fearing judgment. Research has found that mentors and mentees build trust and respect by sharing information, resources, and expectations and by being supportive and collaborative.[12]

On the outskirts of your circle of guidance you should also have friends you trust and talk to. They might not be able to provide guidance because of their lack of experience (assuming they're in the

---

11 "How to Choose a Mentor," It's Your Yale, https://your.yale.edu/work-yale /learn-and-grow/career-development/mentoring/how-choose-mentor.

12 Peter B. Hudson, "Forming the Mentor-Mentee Relationship," *Mentoring & Tutoring: Partnership in Learning* 24, no. 1 (2016): 30–43, https://doi.org/10 .1080/13611267.2016.1163637.

same boat as you), but they can help you process and talk through things you might be stuck on. They will also provide support and join in praying for you.

• • • • •

After getting the green light from my parents, I sought the guidance of my father of confession, who advised me to proceed with prayer and caution. He wanted me to make the right decisions along the way and not rush into anything too quickly. Next, I introduced Mina (Fr. Antony's name before ordination) to my trusted mentor, who had been observing my spiritual growth for years. She had watched me make many mistakes and a few strides in romantic relationships, and she had guided me along the way. I was going down the checklist of my circle of guidance, and this relationship passed with flying colors. But the most critical guidance I needed was from the only one who truly mattered: God. I had one crucial prayer throughout our dating and engagement period, and I didn't stop praying until I walked into the church on our wedding day. I constantly prayed, "God, if this isn't from you, take it away."

It was the same prayer I prayed whenever I was interested in pursuing a romantic relationship with someone. And time and time again, God had answered it by shutting the door on every dating prospect and not allowing it to go anywhere. There were times when I felt the Holy Spirit tugging on my heart, telling me something wasn't right, and other times when my feelings about someone were not reciprocated. Mina was the first person with whom I saw every door opening, and opening with ease. Even as my feelings for him grew deeper, I kept praying that prayer, even if it meant that submitting to God's will would end with heartbreak. I would have rather taken the heartbreak over a life God didn't want for me.

My knowledge of the future was and always will be limited. My feelings can go up and down. My predictions of what Mina might be like as a husband could have been wrong. But God is never wrong. His knowledge is infinite, and He doesn't act on fluctuating feelings. I wanted what He wanted for me. I never wanted to end up in a marriage where I would utter the words, "I chose the wrong person." And choosing the right person was too much pressure to bear on my own. I wanted to seek God's will and discern who the right partner was for me.

Myths about Singleness

Myth #1: I'm a failure if I remain single.

I was once speaking to a concerned mother about her single daughter. The mother told me that her daughter didn't have any luck with dating. Her daughter was an attractive, God-fearing woman in her thirties and well-accomplished. She had been in a few relationships that did not work out. The daughter was starting to make peace with her single state and was genuinely trying to find contentment in it, whether for a season or a lifetime, but her mother said, "I don't want her to give up on finding a spouse." She saw her daughter's satisfaction with singleness as a threat to her chance at marriage.

I challenged the mother to think about the most important thing at stake: her daughter's salvation. She admitted that both the path of singleness and the path of marriage would ultimately lead her daughter to salvation, but because she knew of her daughter's deep desire for marriage, she had formerly only prayed for God to bring her a suitable partner. Now her prayer changed to asking God for the best path for her daughter's salvation.

With all the cultural pressure that exists around marriage, and where major milestones like getting a job, getting married, and having kids, are highly regarded, it's easy to slip into thinking that you've "failed" if you never get married or have kids. But that's simply not true. There is a greater purpose in life than finding a spouse. We all were given a great commandment, "You shall love the LORD your God with all your heart, with all your soul, and with all your strength" (Deut. 6:5). The only failure we have to fear is falling short of loving God and others. Rest assured that your salvation does not depend on your marital status.

Myth #2: Getting into a relationship will solve my problems.

Dating or getting married will not only *not* solve your problems but will come with its own new set of problems. Whether you're struggling with loneliness, insecurity, anxiety, depression, porn addiction, or anything else, these struggles won't go away once you enter a relationship. In fact, your struggles can become more complicated to treat when another person is involved because the consequences of your actions can affect you both. You should get as healthy as you can be standing on your own before leaning on another person.[13] Make your mental and spiritual health a priority before you enter a relationship, because unfortunately, your struggles can even get worse if you are in a relationship or marriage where Christ is not the center and you're neglecting your overall health.

So rather than expecting a relationship to fix your problems, seek help from a mental health counselor or therapist. If you prioritize working on yourself *before* entering into any relationship, your relationship will be stronger! And not only will fighting to overcome

---

13   Emily Brown, "Debra Fileta: The Markers of a Healthy Relationship," *Relevant*, February 8, 2022, https://relevantmagazine.com/life5/new-you /debra-fileta-the-markers-of-a-healthy-relationship/.

these problems strengthen your relationships, it will also build resiliency in you. Each struggle will sanctify you and bring you closer to God. Your problems might feel like heavy crosses to carry, but those crosses refine us to depend on God more than we rely on ourselves or anyone else.

Myth #3: I'm incomplete without a significant other.

The only person you should feel incomplete without is Christ Himself. Another human cannot complete you; our identity is in Christ alone. When we rely on a partner to make us feel complete, they will always fall short because that is God's role. Creating an expectation for someone to complete us is a lot of pressure, and we are signing them up for a commitment they cannot fulfill. Some feelings of joy and fulfillment do come from being in a healthy relationship, but ultimately, maximum joy and fulfillment come from drawing closer to God.

Additionally, our purpose in life is far greater than having a significant other. God can use you as a chosen vessel for His glory regardless of your marital state. Whether there is a ring on your finger or not, you are a complete and whole person.

2

Prepare to Date

When dating is your process for finding the right spouse for marriage, preparing for dating is one way to prepare for marriage. There are a few ways to prepare yourself for dating, which will be discussed in this chapter, but first let's look at the bigger picture of preparing for a godly marriage.

The necessity of preparing for marriage is not a man-made concept, and it's more than just wedding planning—it can be traced all the way back to Genesis. At the beginning of the Creation story, we see God beautifully creating heaven and earth, separating light and darkness, and fashioning waters and land to fill them with all kinds of creatures. He meticulously thought out the order of creation and saved the best for last, creating man and woman in the image of the Trinity.

When Adam lived in the garden, he first had a direct relationship with God. After establishing this important relationship, there was another critical step God took with Adam before He brought Eve to him. In Genesis 2:15, we see how "the LORD God took the man and put him in the garden of Eden to tend and keep it." So

Adam had responsibilities to attend to; he was in charge of tending the garden and naming each living creature. While he carried out his responsibilities, Adam heeded God's commandment of staying away from the tree of the knowledge of good and evil. He walked in the garden as a fellow worker with God, having direct access to Him and caring after His creation. But in all of creation, there was no helper found comparable to him, so God caused Adam to fall into a deep sleep, made a woman out of his rib, and declared they were now one flesh.

Notice how God prepared Adam before He created Eve for him: God gave him a job. Adam had to figure out how to take care of himself and maintain his responsibilities before caring for a wife. This was also after establishing a direct relationship with one another. Then God made Eve for Adam and established the law of marriage. Likewise, before entering a marriage, there are steps we can take to be ready to receive the spouse God has for us. And before setting out to meet our spouse, we can prepare ourselves for that dating process.

When to Wait and When to Date

It was the summer of my junior year in high school, and a group of about two hundred high school girls was gathered at the annual ECCYC (East Coast Coptic Youth Convention). A panel of priests and youth leaders sat on the stage, and it was time for Q&A. I sent in a question that read, "At what age can I start dating?" I desperately wanted an answer: a number to look forward to or an age I could start counting down to. But to my disappointment, the panel of experts left me without one, and rightly so. Dating readiness is not one-size-fits-all. There is no age that, once reached, would magically grant a person enough maturity to be able to date.

I was struggling to wait for the right time to date because I saw dating as a fun thing to do. Everyone around me—from friends in school to the general media—made dating seem like the ultimate happy place, and I was becoming impatient. I wanted it to be my time to be happy. I had a one-dimensional view of dating: that it was my time to receive—to receive love from a significant other, care from someone, and the validation I was seeking. I wanted to escape feelings of loneliness, and I thought that having a partner would indeed do just that.

I failed to realize the more profound meaning behind and reason for dating. But as I matured, I realized that there was more to dating than short-term happiness. Dating was the means of getting to know someone and determining if they could be your lifelong partner. And dating had to come after I knew myself well enough to know what kind of partner I would match with; for me, high school certainly wasn't the right time for that.

Fast forward some years later, and I am now a married youth leader on similar Q&A panels. I love speaking to teens about relationships and dating, emphasizing the waiting phase. The number one question I typically get from teens is, "When can I start dating?" They don't usually like the answer, as I also didn't like it when I was their age. I tell them the answer requires a lot of self-reflection and a few more years of waiting. But if you've spent some time waiting and reflecting, how do you know when you are ready to date? Here are some things to keep in mind.

Maturity

The majority of teenagers, and even some young adults, do not yet have the maturity needed for a long-term relationship that leads to marriage. But not everyone reaches the same maturity level at the same age; scientific research has tried to pinpoint this phenomenon. A study found that the development and maturation of the prefrontal cortex, the area of the brain which regulates our thoughts, actions, and emotions, occurs primarily during adolescence but isn't fully accomplished until the age of twenty-five.[14] The prefrontal cortex is known to be one of the last regions of the brain to reach full development, and it has a major influence on our decision-making abilities. This makes the adolescent brain vulnerable to environmental stress, risky behavior, drug addiction, impaired driving, and unprotected sex. And while dating might not be as high stakes as these behaviors, it still requires that people be mature enough to make the right decisions and avoid regrettable mistakes.

Another study was done across eleven countries with over five thousand participants aged ten to thirty, and it found a difference in cognitive capacity and psychosocial maturity between adolescents and adults.[15] Cognitive capacity is the basis of logical thinking, while psychosocial maturity is the ability to restrain yourself in the face of emotional, exciting, or risky stimuli. The study found that cognitive capacity reached adult levels around age sixteen, and psychosocial maturity reached adult levels beyond age eighteen. Both cognitive capacity and psychosocial maturity are important when it comes to dating, as making good decisions and having self-control

---

14 Mariam Arain et al., "Maturation of the Adolescent Brain," *Neuropsychiatric Disease and Treatment* 2013, no. 9 (April 3, 2013): 449, https://doi.org/10.2147/ndt.s39776.

15 Grace Icenogle, Laurence Steinberg, Natasha Duell, Jason Chein, Lei Chang, Nandita Chaudhary, Laura Di Giunta, et al., "Adolescents' Cognitive Capacity Reaches Adult Levels Prior to Their Psychosocial Maturity: Evidence for a 'Maturity Gap' in a Multinational, Cross-Sectional Sample," *Law and Human Behavior* 43, no. 1 (2019): 69–85, https://doi.org/10.1037/lhb0000315.

will enhance your dating experience and not having these abilities will deprive it of success.

To gauge your own current level of brain maturity, reflect on how you interact with others and how you handle moments of peer pressure. Are your interactions logical and your emotional responses within reason? Are you able to resist negative peer pressure and not act on impulse? If you are not able to tell if you have the maturity to start dating, your circle of guidance can help you discern it.

With maturity also comes a level of self-awareness that is fundamental to being able to engage in a healthy romantic relationship. Self-awareness allows you to recognize where your emotions, feelings, and actions are coming from. It also helps you accurately assess your strengths and weaknesses without being misled by your ego. These things allow you to be more knowledgeable about what you bring to the table in a relationship, whether it's positive or negative, which helps you understand what flaws you need to work on before or while you are in a committed relationship. Self-awareness can be gained by careful and consistent self-examination and reflection as well as through the feedback you get from your close relationships with others. For example, as you interact with your loved ones or circle of guidance, they might point out things in your personality you are not aware of, which gives you the opportunity to work on improvement.

· · · · ·

In addition to maturity and self-awareness, there are three relationships in your life you need to focus on in order to prepare yourself for a healthy romantic relationship. Matthew 22:37–40 shows us what these are. Here, when one of the Pharisees asks Christ what is the greatest commandment, He answers: "'You shall love the LORD your God with all your heart, with all your soul, and with all your mind.' This is *the* first and great commandment. And *the* second *is* like it: 'You shall love your neighbor as yourself.' On these two commandments hang all the Law and the Prophets." From these verses, we can draw three conclusions. First, we must love God with every part of our being. Second, we have to love our neighbor. And last, we must love ourselves, and from that, we can love our neighbor. These commandments show us the importance of love in three essential relationships: our relationship with God, with our neighbor, and with ourselves.

Our Relationship with God

If you grew up watching romantic movies as I did, then you're very familiar with the typical plot. It goes something like this: boy meets girl, boy and girl can't be together because of some obstacle, they find a way to overcome that obstacle, get married, and ride off in their horse and carriage to live happily ever after. That makes for a nice, feel-good movie, but it couldn't be further from reality. Those movies only highlight the romantic chase, and once the man wins over the woman with his charm and romantic gestures, it's a happy ending. But in real life that's only the beginning.

The movies don't go on to show you the hard side of relationships, when partners need grit and tenacity to move the relationship forward. True love grows deep roots over time as it is tried and tested; it has good days, but bad days too. It requires the hard work of patience, kindness, selflessness, long-suffering, and sacrifice (1 Cor. 13:4–8). And this kind of love can only be learned from Christ, the truest example of love. Christ entered our broken world and showed us how we ought to love one another, even to the point of death. He showed us this by coming not to condemn us but by making

"Himself of no reputation, taking the form of a bondservant, *and* coming in the likeness of men. And being found in appearance as a man, He humbled Himself and became obedient to *the point of death*, even the death of the cross" (Phil. 2:7–8). Thus, loving God first is a prerequisite for loving a significant other (although our love for God is ever growing and never complete).

This type of sacrificial love is especially important in our relationship with our partner because close relationships have a way of bringing flaws to light. Our partners see our faults, weaknesses, and many blemishes, and we see theirs. While we are dating, those flaws will begin to surface, and if we choose to move from dating to marriage, we'll have to be ready to love our partner despite their shortcomings, as our heavenly Father does with us. As spouses, we don't just see our partner's physical nakedness but also the nakedness of each other's souls. And because of our flaws, we will hurt one another at times, but we forgive and give grace to our partners when they hurt us, the same way the Lord offers us grace and forgiveness every time we sin. However, we cannot show grace to our partner unless we are first filled with His grace. What grace would we be able to offer if we were drawing from an empty well? So make God the foundation of any relationship you build. Make Him the center of your partnership, draw from His unconditional love, and you will never run out.

• • • • •

Knowing that this kind of love is essential for a relationship, it's important to spend time growing in intimacy with God and learning what this love looks like. As you prepare to date, the time you have to yourself is best utilized by building a relationship with God when you can afford for this to be your only focus—because as we mentioned in an earlier chapter, marriage (and being in a relationship with someone) introduces a new set of cares and concerns that is not present when you are single.

There are several practices you can incorporate into your routine to help you draw nearer to God:

- Read Scripture, which allows you to hear God's message and receive His wisdom.
- Engage in regular, consistent, and even structured prayer (e.g. using the *Book of Hours*), which keeps you in open dialogue with the Savior throughout the day.
- Meditate and reflect, which are practices that allow you to be still and invite peace and an awareness of God's presence in your life.
- Serve others by participating in ministries, which will allow you to experience the love God has for humanity.
- Have a practice of gratitude, which opens your eyes to God's generosity and His compassion for you.

The resources that will help you foster a deep, loving, genuine relationship with God are plentiful and readily available. Actively seek how you may make this precious investment, one that will continue to support you when distractions come.

If you seek God and make Him the primary priority of the relationship, everything will fall into place. Don't just take my word for it: Christ Himself said, "But seek first the kingdom of God and His righteousness, and all these things shall be added to you" (Matt. 6:33). Develop a relationship with Him that's deep and personal because the closer you are to Him, the more you will be like Him and be able to emulate His love, not just for your partner but for others as well.

Our Relationship with Our Neighbor

God built us with a desire not just to connect with Him but also with one another, and that's why He commands us to love our neighbor as well. The command to love Him comes first, because our love for Him then spills over naturally into loving others. But loving others also takes work and practice, and learning how to love others is a stepping stone to loving a significant other. When we love others as Christ commands us, we exercise muscles that are key to successful relationships. We will have the opportunity to practice kindness, compassion, patience, humility, forgiveness, and sacrifice, and we will gain experience navigating various challenging situations in relationships such as resolving conflict, communicating openly, and showing up when needed. As we interact with others, we also become able to identify the types of personalities we get along with and which ones we want to steer away from. Carrying all this knowledge and experience into a romantic relationship will be tremendously helpful.

Additionally, being surrounded by people who look out for you and who model Christian love (including your circle of guidance, as discussed earlier) can strengthen your dating or marital relationship. They will become an example you can look up to and model your own relationship after. When your friends have values that align with yours and with Scripture, you ensure that you have a community in place that will support the growth of your relationship—or that will give you wise counsel if you're in a dating relationship that's not good for you. This community can also keep you accountable in practicing Christian love the right way.

Another important function your community has is that your perception of what is acceptable and normal is shaped by who you surround yourself with. If you are surrounded by those who are accustomed to being deceitful, selfish, or excessively combative with their own partners, this might set unhealthy expectations for you. Alternately, if you're immersed in a community where godly interactions are encouraged and strived after you will be more likely to do the same. Honesty, selflessness, and peacemaking will be the normative behaviors you engage in.

. . . . .

Unfortunately, it can be difficult to find a strong community and a circle of guidance in the US today. Jennie Allen, in her book *Find Your People,* examines how the majority of people in the world live in communities, while in the US individuals tend to live alone and feel isolated from loved ones,[16] because proximity to loved ones has become lower on the list of priorities when we determine where to live and work. Unlike much of the rest of the world, we don't typically live within a reasonable distance from our friends and family where we can walk over and knock on their front door. We also tend to use services that bring what we need right to our door, such as ordering things on Amazon instead of going to a store and interacting with others, or using a meal-delivery service instead of asking a loved one to go out to dinner. This robs us of opportunities to go out and interact with our community. Social media has also contributed to this problem by providing a way to socialize while alone at home—but these end up being shallow connections that fall short of deep relationships.

Instead, we need to form meaningful connections in order to create our community. But how do we cultivate deep relationships in a society that's built for the opposite? Start with your church community: get involved in your local parish and get to know people who

---

16   Jennie Allen, *Find Your People: Building Deep Community in a Lonely World* (Colorado Springs, CO: WaterBrook, 2022), 12.

already share your faith and values. You can also join a club for any hobbies you're interested in (for example, a book club, hiking group, gardening club, or adult sports league). Or you can volunteer your time to a cause that you care about, which is another way to find people you already have something in common with. Additionally, you can get to know your classmates or coworkers to see if there is potential for good friendships there. These are just a few ways to find people that you can love as your neighbor. Try brainstorming a list of other ways to do so that are available where you live!

Our Relationship with Ourself

In order to love our future significant other, it's important to create a healthy relationship with ourselves by learning to love and esteem ourselves. And this is not an arrogant or narcissistic type of self-love but a humble one where we understand that God deeply loves *all* His people, including us, and as God's beloved children, we are worthy to receive love just as all people are worthy. The Bible tells us how God deeply loves us, just as the popular verse says, "For God so loved the world that He gave His only begotten Son, that whoever believes in Him should not perish but have everlasting life" (John 3:16). And in Psalm 8 we read:

> What is man that You are mindful of him,
> And the son of man that You visit him?
> For You have made him a little lower than the angels,
> And You have crowned him with glory and honor. (vv. 4–5)

So it's important to show love and care for ourselves *just because God wants us to love and care for all of His creation, including our own selves*—but also, if we don't know how to love ourselves then we will be unable to love others. For one thing, if we don't see our own value, we may fail to see the value of others as well: we may treat everyone as if they are as unworthy of love as we believe ourselves to be. On another practical level, if we do not love and care for our soul and body, we will not be able to show up for others in the right mental and physical state when they need us. When we neglect ourselves, we will have a hard time being there for others and loving them well.

Learning to love ourselves also contributes to building our self-esteem, which is important for maintaining healthy relationships with others because if we do not love ourselves and understand our true worth as a child of God, we'll look to others for validation. We'll start measuring our self-worth by how much someone else loves us and cares for us, and this is dangerous because people are flawed and inconsistent and can't give us the constant and perfect love we need. That can only come from God and from loving ourselves as He loves us. Research even shows that if we highly value how others see us, it leads to lower self-esteem.[17] And when our self-esteem is compromised, we might end up settling for anyone who makes us feel loved even in the slightest. Take a look at Mariana and her struggle, for example.

Mariana was a beautiful young woman, yet every time she looked in the mirror she saw one more thing she wanted to fix. Compared with the images of women she saw on her screens, she wasn't as picture-perfect as she wanted to be. Growing up in a broken household also didn't help her self-esteem. Her dad had been absent most of her life, and she never received the love every little girl longs for

---

17   Katherine Rimes, Patrick Smith, and Livia Bridge, "Low Self-Esteem: A Refined Cognitive Behavioural Model," *Behavioural and Cognitive Psychotherapy* 51, no. 6 (November 2023): 579–594, https://pubmed.ncbi.nlm.nih .gov/37170762/.

from a father. She also had no other father figure to give her the affection and care she needed.

When Mariana got older and began to catch the attention of guys, she enjoyed hearing their sweet words of admiration. The whispers of love she heard filled her heart with happiness, but that happiness never lasted long and she found herself in an unhealthy cycle of dating one guy after another. One would promise her love and commitment, and she'd gradually compromise her values for him, in order to keep his love, and soon after, he'd walk away. Then another would swoop in and promise to heal her broken heart, but in the process leave her heart broken again. Each guy's flattery would easily win her over. She looked to these men to feel seen. She wanted to be worthy of their love. *Am I worth anything if I don't have someone to love me?* She often wondered.

Mariana lacked a deep sense of self-love; she was trying to fill an emptiness that no partner could fill. It wasn't until she started to see herself through the eyes of Christ that she began her long journey of healing. She began to realize that the love she longed for was the love of the true Father, and that until she could take hold of that, she wouldn't be able to love herself—or anyone else—properly.

Mariana isn't the only person to find herself in this predicament. Many studies have found that girls who grew up with an absent father are more likely to be sexually promiscuous.[18] But it's important to keep in mind that even if our earthly fathers fail us, our heavenly Father never will. In fact, He will show up in more ways than any biological father ever could.

Through my ministry with teen girls and young women, I've seen certain patterns that can occur when they seek validation

---

18   Sarah E. Hill et al., "Absent Fathers and Sexual Strategies," *The Psychologist*, May 6, 2016, https://www.bps.org.uk/psychologist/absent-fathers-and-sexual-strategies.

from the opposite sex. If a young woman is struggling to accept and like herself and she is flooded by compliments from a guy, she will often slowly let her guard down. When she doesn't feel like she measures up to everyone else, and someone comes in and makes her feel valuable, easing her insecurities, she becomes awe-struck with him and follows him, even if he may be on a path away from Christ. If he is of a different faith or spiritual standing, he will become a wedge between her and Christ. Along the way, she compromises her faith values to make the relationship work, and she is led further away from God, not closer. The same is true for men who seek validation from women. A person of any gender who is not confident in who they are, and is lacking self-love, will abandon parts of their identity if it means receiving love from a significant other.

Girls might think that being in a relationship will raise their self-esteem, but research has proven the opposite is actually true. One study showed that among high school students who are dating, girls who were in previous relationships and continue to date had the lowest self-esteem scores.[19] The girls with the highest self-esteem scores were those who had previously been in relationships and had stopped dating. Across the study, both boys and girls who were dating experienced lower self-esteem.

The love you need to raise your self-esteem, fill your insecurities, and understand your true worth is not the love of another person but the love of Christ. Look at the story of the Samaritan woman and how Christ's love transformed her (John 4:1–30). This woman went to draw water from the well at the most undesirable time of the day, likely so she would not run into anyone, because she was

---

19   Donna L. McDonald and John Paul McKinney, "Steady Dating and Self-Esteem in High School Students," *Journal of Adolescence* 17, no. 6 (December 1994): 557–64, https://doi.org/10.1006/jado.1994.1049.

embarrassed about her sexual lifestyle. Christ went out of His way to meet her at that well and requested a drink from her, striking up a conversation. When He asked her about her husband, she didn't give Him the whole story, but He knew it anyway. She could hardly contain her joy when she realized she was speaking to the Messiah and found Him showering her with love and forgiveness. She wanted others to experience what she experienced, so she ran to the people of Samaria and told them about Christ, "and many of the Samaritans of that city believed in Him because of the word of the woman who testified, 'He told me all that I *ever* did'" (John 4:39). Through His gentle and loving way, He made her new. There is no doubt that her self-love and love for God grew tremendously through that experience.

So don't let the enemy whisper lies in your ear and make you doubt God's love for you. The enemy likes to do this by reminding us of our past mistakes and by convincing us that our imperfections and flaws make us unworthy of God's love. If remembering your sins stops you from loving yourself, know that this is from Satan and not God. Because once you've repented and confessed, your sins are forgiven, and you're as good as new, as we read in 2 Corinthians 5:17, "Therefore, if anyone *is* in Christ, he *is* a new creation; old things have passed away; behold, all things have become new." If you're struggling to love yourself as a child of God, you can contemplate the things God says about us: you are the apple of His eye, hidden under the shadow of His wings (Ps. 17:8), you are His workmanship (Eph. 2:10), fearfully and wonderfully made (Ps. 139:14), and you are His (Is. 43:1).

If, at times, you feel unlovable, it might be time to start forgiving yourself. Why are you still punishing yourself if the Almighty Judge already forgave you? Lift your head high and walk confidently, knowing that forgiveness renews all, and from that, you can start or continue on your path of self-love. Draw your self-love from God because He is the one unchanging thing in your life. Your feelings and circumstances can change and threaten your happiness, but God's character and goodness will never change. No one else can match the love He offers; once you have that, you can begin to love others well.

Myths about Waiting

Myth #1: I need to date this person so I don't lose them to someone else.

Sometimes two people start a relationship prematurely because they're afraid they'll lose the person they like to someone else (I often see this with teenagers). But trying to control the outcome of a situation is God's job, not ours. There is a beautiful synergy between our free will and God's will. We prayerfully seek God's will for us while wisely discerning the right choice to make.

If you meet someone you think could be your future spouse and are not ready to be in a relationship in your current stage in life, take that as an opportunity to form a friendship with them. Make sure you have healthy boundaries in place so that the friendship doesn't look like a romantic relationship. When I first met my husband, I was a freshman in college and not ready to be in a serious relationship. It wasn't until three years later that we started dating. It would have been the wrong time if we dated immediately and tried planting a relationship that wasn't ready to bear fruit.

I know many other people who met their future spouse years before they were ready and started nothing romantically with each other. But God brought that person back into their life at the right time. Trust in God's timing and be brave enough to let someone go if it's not the right time for you.

I firmly believe in God's divine providence for the timing of when He brings other people into your life. You might be ready to date, but God could still be working on your future partner. You might think you're ready to date, but God wants you to wait a little longer so you can be better prepared. You might be getting impatient and tired of waiting, but God wants you to trust Him fully and not take matters into your own hands. His plan is always better than anything we could ever plan. He sees our past, present, and future all at once. His vision is far greater than ours, as Isaiah the prophet writes:

"For My thoughts *are* not your thoughts,
Nor *are* your ways My ways," says the LORD.
"For *as* the heavens are higher than the earth,
So are My ways higher than your ways,
And My thoughts than your thoughts." (Is. 55:8–9)

Myth #2: There's no harm in dating early.

Starting a relationship before you're ready can actually result in more harm than good. I once coached a young man who had begun dating at a young age because he met a girl he was attracted to and didn't see the point in waiting if he knew he wanted to be with her. He kept this relationship a secret, knowing his circle of guidance would disapprove. Unfortunately, he found himself in a toxic relationship, as his girlfriend would treat him well one day and terribly the next (more on this in chapter 5). But he told himself that relationships are hard sometimes and they require work. On his own, he could not tell the difference between a healthy and unhealthy relationship.

He was also physically involved with her, and the pleasure that came with it kept him returning to her despite how awfully she treated him at times. This relationship lasted longer than it should have, leaving him with much emotional damage he had to undo. When he got older, he wanted to settle down and be in a serious, committed relationship, but every time he started dating someone, he doubted his judgment. He feared history would repeat itself and he would end up in another damaging relationship. This fear was crippling him and he couldn't move forward with any relationship, which is why he sought coaching.

He realized that he could have avoided the aftermath he was dealing with if he had avoided dating prematurely. Nevertheless, he knew with the right approach he could work through his fears and have a healthy mindset toward dating. He trusted in God's grace and was willing to put in the hard work for healing to occur. After preparing himself properly this time by reframing his mindset around dating, involving his circle of guidance, and putting God first, he met a lovely young woman he dated and eventually married.

I share this story with you to encourage you to wait until you are ready to date, and one sign of that is your comfort with being honest with your circle of guidance. If you're afraid to tell them about your dating life, it might mean it's not the right time or you're simply not ready. I also want you to avoid the heartache that comes with dating prematurely and being with the wrong person. Don't let your emotions and desires push you to jump into dating before you're ready.

Myth #3: Everyone around me is dating, so I will date to not be left out.

When you are surrounded by peers who are dating, and at times are the only single one among your friends, you may naturally feel like you're left out. This becomes increasingly noticeable when you're older and those relationships turn into engagements and marriages while you remain single. It can make you feel lonely and question your relationship status. Wrestling with feelings of loneliness is no easy battle, and it's okay to feel those feelings. But don't let them overwhelm you to the point that you abandon hope. Remember that everyone is on a different timeline.

Just because it seems like everyone your age is dating, that doesn't mean you are also ready to date. Don't let peer pressure or self-pressure lead you to start something you're not ready for, especially if you're in your teen years. Even as a young adult, you may journey into dating at a different time than your peers. Dating before you're ready can shift your priorities, and not always in the favor of your overall success. Juggling your needs is tough enough, so adding the needs of someone else when you're not at a steady place can put a strain on your well-being.

For a relationship to work, both partners have to be ready. Focusing on your readiness is the best thing you can do for your future relationship. You should be mature and standing firm on a foundation built from having a growing relationship with God, others, and yourself. Having the right spiritual footing, an awareness of who you are, and guidance from those closest to you will help you discern the right time to start dating. When it comes to dating, readiness matters.

PART 2

The Dating

3

Date to Find a Mate

How do you know when you're ready to start your dating journey? You are ready to start once you've discerned that marriage is your path, and once you've prepared yourself for dating by understanding what true Christian love looks like. You'll need to have developed a strong relationship with God, others, and yourself, and have the right level of maturity. In this chapter, we will examine *why* to date and how to figure out *who* to date, to better equip you for this adventure.

If you grew up in the 1990s or early 2000s as a Christian in the West, (and even if you grew up Orthodox) you were most likely influenced by the evangelical purity culture movement—or if you were born later, your current youth leaders likely were.[20] You would have been taught that premarital sex was a great sin and physical purity carried significant weight (both those claims are biblically

---

20 Julie Ingersoll, "How the 'Extreme Abstinence' of the Purity Movement Created a Sense of Shame in Evangelical Women," *The Conversation*, December 10, 2019, https://theconversation.com/how-the-extreme -abstinence-of-the-purity-movement-created-a-sense-of-shame-in -evangelical-women-127589.

valid), but you also would have learned a few flawed teachings. You might have been encouraged to ditch dating completely, as the best-selling book *I Kissed Dating Goodbye* (Multnomah Books, 1997) advised. Purity culture claimed that dating could lead to sinful temptations, so avoiding it helped protect your purity. It placed dating in the "ungodly" category, and you only had two options: platonic friendship or serious dating, referred to as courting. These ideas put intense pressure on any relationship you started and created a stigma around dating.

According to this movement, what would happen when you met someone you were romantically interested in? Before even asking them out, you would have to be sure this was the person you wanted to court. But how could you be sure you wanted to be in a serious relationship with someone unless you got to know them a little more first? This is where embarking on the adventure of dating becomes useful.

Why Date?

Contrary to the messages of purity culture, Christian dating can be done in a way that honors God and others. But how do we do this? For one thing, Christians shouldn't date in a selfish way, chasing after sexual gratification and acting impulsively, only looking out for their own interest. Additionally, romantic relationships don't have to lead to the compromise of your purity and Christian values. Christians must do the hard work of deciphering between modern secular dating, which can be self-centered and confusing, and godly dating, which should be Christ-centered and clear. Keep in mind that God will be as involved as you let Him be in your dating life.

It's also critical to figure out your own purpose for dating before you set out to date and to make sure your purpose fits with God's purpose for your life. Your reason for dating will make a difference in how you go about it and the results it yields. If you're dating just for fun, to fill up your free time, or to avoid loneliness, your relationships will look different than if you are dating to find a lifelong partner. Your level of seriousness and commitment might be lacking in the former. While you don't have to marry the person you're dating, it's good to focus on dating as the pathway to marriage. But while marriage should be the end goal of dating in general, it doesn't have to be the result of every relationship. Relationships help you explore the possibility of marriage with the person you're dating.

Knowing where you stand before entering a relationship with someone else is essential. Both people must be on the same page and understand the purpose of the dating relationship. Don't let too much time pass before finding out what kind of relationship the other person is looking for. If your goals aren't aligned, it's better to find out sooner rather than later. And along the way, you should treat each other with love and kindness, intending the best for the person you're dating whether you decide to move forward or break up. You don't want to leave each other worse than how you found each other. But don't mistake this for seeing someone as a project you want to fix and improve. That is an unhealthy way of dating and plays into the savior complex, which is not your role; that role only belongs to God.

Dating is the journey you take while looking for a compatible partner who will fit into your life as effortlessly as possible. Whether you start as strangers or have an established friendship, the time you take to build a solid friendship in the beginning will be the foundation for a strong relationship later on. Things should generally go smoothly at the beginning of the relationship, or what some like to call the honeymoon phase. There will always be a level of effort required in meshing two worlds together, but if there are major challenges and roadblocks from day one, it might be a sign that something isn't right. Then, as you go deeper into the relationship, get ready to roll up your sleeves because this is where the real work begins.

Who to Date

Now that you have a clear understanding of the purpose of dating, the next step is to know what you're looking for well before you start dating. Not knowing what you're looking for while dating is like going to the grocery store without a grocery list, wasting time going up and down the aisles, buying things that look good to your hungry eyes, and hoping they'll make a delicious meal when you get home. Unless you're a top-rated chef, the chance that you'll make anything resembling a gourmet meal without the right groceries and instructions is slim. Knowing what makes a Christian marriage thrive and looking for those traits in a partner is like having a proven recipe and the shopping list you need to make that satisfying meal.

When you first meet someone you are interested in dating, you might mistake having butterflies in your stomach, a racing heart, or feeling smitten as signs that you've found the right person. But in reality, those are fleeting emotions you might experience just because you are infatuated with someone—or even when you're in the presence of someone you should be careful around because of the strong attraction you have to them. Don't believe in the widely popular myth of love at first sight. Research has shown that love at first sight is not a real form of love but is nothing more than a strong initial attraction.[21] Real love grows over time and is not something you can feel immediately.

---

21 Florian Zsok et al., "What Kind of Love Is Love at First Sight? An Empirical Investigation," *Personal Relationships* 24, no. 4 (November 17, 2017): 869–85, https://doi.org/10.1111/pere.12218.

So instead of opening yourself up to letting those butterflies carry you away, before you set out looking for the "one" you need to identify what qualities this person should possess. To help identify whether you are ready to start dating, ask yourself these questions: Do you know what you're looking for in a lifelong partner? Or will you be distracted by anyone attractive who comes your way? Have you considered what is needed to make a marriage work, specifically with your personality, your faith, values, etc.? And how can someone fit into the picture of the life you envision for yourself? Unless you know the answers to those questions, you'll wander aimlessly trying to find the right person. Saint John Chrysostom shows us how this can work:

> If we investigate these laws [God's laws for marriage] and know them well before we marry, we will take care to choose a wife who is well-ordered from the beginning and compatible with our character. If we marry a woman like this, we will gain not only the benefit that we will never divorce her, but also that we will love her intensely, as Paul commands.[22]

The person you find should match your current life and where you're heading. You shouldn't have to change who you are or try to change them so that you are compatible with each other. You'll already have the same core beliefs, values, and life goals and can help one another reach those goals. How you see the world should align with each other in various areas of life (see chapter 5 for more on compatibility).

When I work with a client who is single and needs help finding a partner, I encourage them to make a list of qualities, traits,

---

22   Chrysostom, *On Marriage & Family Life,* 91.

and characteristics they're looking for. This list isn't meant to be a list of strict requirements but rather a guide as they begin to date. If they find themselves dating someone who lacks the majority of the qualities they're looking for, the list would indicate it's time to let go. And there must be a correct understanding of what traits belong on this list: this shouldn't be a superficial list, or a list of only physical qualities. Attraction is multifaceted, and physical attraction is only one part of the equation. Intellectual and spiritual attraction should also play a significant role in how you're drawn to a person.

Physical Attraction

I don't recommend being very specific about physical attributes on your list. Beauty comes in all shapes and sizes, so instead of listing the typical traits of outward beauty our society values (e.g., being tall, dark, and handsome), look for someone who lives a healthy lifestyle, takes care of their body, and doesn't chase vanity. And if you're not physically attracted to someone immediately but are drawn to them in other ways; give it some time. Your attraction to them might grow as you learn more about them and see all facets of their personality. Be open to dating people who don't meet your typical criteria; the results might surprise you.

Physical beauty is the first thing to fade over time and, therefore, probably one of the less significant forms of attraction, as Proverbs 31:30 puts it, "beauty *is* passing." The person's spiritual and intellectual attributes will be present for the long haul, and they are the building blocks of a relationship. I'm not saying you should end up with someone you're not physically attracted to. Attraction is important and should be present in a relationship, but don't dismiss someone right away if they look different from the picture you imagined.

The situation with my former client, Amy, illustrates this point well. "He's a great guy, but I'm not very attracted to him," Amy told me. She was at the beginning phase of dating a guy who seemed to have all the qualities she was looking for in a partner, except he didn't look like the other guys she had been attracted to in the past. Although Amy didn't feel that instant attraction, I proposed that she not jump to conclusions early on in dating, and she decided to get to know him a little more. A few months later, she checked in to tell me how great things were going and how her attraction for him grew tremendously as she saw different sides of his personality. Their relationship was heading toward engagement, and today they are happily married. Had Amy dismissed him right away based on physical attraction, she would have missed out on finding a wonderful husband.

The opposite is also true: you can be immediately attracted to someone who is not the right person for you. In fact, when you find yourself deeply admiring someone because of your strong attraction to them, you are most likely infatuated with them. The dictionary defines infatuation as "strong and unreasoning attachment,"[23] and in these cases you may know little to no facts about the person you're infatuated with and your feelings are merely driven by physical attraction. Be aware that infatuation can have a strong grip on your emotions and actions, and therefore, must be controlled wisely. Allow yourself to get to know the person you're admiring objectively and allow logic to lead your decision-making, not just feelings.

---

23 *Merriam-Webster*, s.v. "infatuation (n.)," accessed March 26, 2024, https://www.merriam-webster.com/dictionary/infatuation.

Intellectual Attraction

Being able to have intellectually stimulating dialog with a partner is an important aspect of a relationship. In order to gauge this, you'll need to spend a good amount of time in conversation. Being able to discuss similar interest in books, movies, music, news, or anything that fascinates you creates riveting conversations. Additionally, if our partner can challenge us about certain ideas and engage with us in debates, that can help us grow intellectually and broaden our mind.

Intellectual attraction can come through many different avenues. While sometimes someone's career might be a good gauge of their intellect, it's not always the best indicator. So refrain from putting a specific job title on your list; instead, ask yourself why you're looking for someone with that particular career. It could be that you want someone hardworking, ambitious, and successful—and those qualities are present in a variety of careers. If you're looking for someone who has an academic education that matches yours, consider that a person with an entrepreneurial background and less education might also be a good fit. If you care about financial stability, remember that someone can find this through various ventures and that it can disappear in hard times, but someone who is hardworking will always find ways to regain it.

Examine the kind of attention a person gives to their career because it can tell you a lot about them. Are they obsessed with their job and willingly spend extra, long hours there? Then you might be dealing with someone who is a workaholic. Are they chasing after money and will sacrifice anything to earn it? That might be someone who is serving the wrong kind of master, as Matthew 6:24 says, "No one can serve two masters; for either he will hate the one and love the other, or else he will be loyal to the one and despise the other. You cannot serve God and mammon." Some people live to work, and others work to live. Which one are you looking for?

You might also be dating someone who does not yet have a job or a well-defined career. They might be a student still figuring out their career path, or they are just uncertain as to which direction they want to go. Yet you can still have strong intellectual attraction with one another. Their sense of purpose, ambition, and goals can be present before an actual job is. For example, when my husband and I started dating, neither of us had a full-time job. I was interning between college semesters, and he was attending seminary with a side job that he occasionally clocked into. We both started full-time jobs a few short months before our wedding, yet before that we knew what kind of work ethic the other possessed. Also, our intellectual attraction went beyond what we both did for a living; it revolved around our interest in similar subjects and love of reading. We always had something to discuss, teach each other, and debate.

Spiritual Attraction

On paper, Donna was the dream girl Alex had been looking for. She was attractive, involved in her local parish, and had an excellent corporate job. They shared the same values and core beliefs. After just a few dates, Alex had already started picturing his life with Donna. Then the initial excitement of the relationship began to wear off, and he started noticing her inconsistent behaviors. She was rude to restaurant waitstaff when they dined out, insisting that the customer was always right. She wasn't always truthful in her job and slacked off when no one was looking. Alex noticed she was only eager to attend church for social gatherings, and she wanted to skip the long liturgical services. She would often show up late on Sundays and make it just in time to teach her Sunday school class, and her spiritual practices of Bible reading and prayer began to take a backseat as she spent more time with Alex.

Alex was the opposite. His behavior matched his values and he was a kind and honest person. He cared deeply about his relationship with God and let nothing get in the way. He was punctual when he arrived at church services, eager to benefit from the sacramental gifts. All the things he initially found attractive in Donna began to fade away as he became unimpressed with the spiritual life she led. He thought she was the God-fearing woman she described herself as, and she might have been indeed, but not to the level Alex was looking for. He wasn't judging her character and viewing her in a negative way. He was simply analyzing, without casting judgment, whether they would be compatible.

A common characteristic I typically see on people's lists is that they want someone who is God-fearing. But that means different things to different people. To some, it means someone who occasionally attends church services and follows basic Christian ethics—they don't lie, cheat, or steal. To others, it means someone who is committed to the liturgical life of the Church and is immersed in ministry. Alex and Donna were clearly on different pages regarding what they considered God-fearing.

It's important to look for someone who has (or is willing to have) the same level of commitment as you. The depth of someone's relationship with God should be somewhat equal to yours. You don't want to find yourself unequally yoked with someone (see 2 Cor. 6:14); if you're someone who strictly observes the fasts and feasts of the Church but you are dating someone who only shows up to the Christmas and Easter services, there's a great chance you'll be unequally yoked in the relationship.

And be careful not to be fooled by someone's outward activities. Someone can be a devoted deacon, reader, or cantor with a lovely voice but have no real relationship with God and instead, seeks the praise of others. Someone can be a dedicated youth ministry leader trying to bring others to Christ while they themselves are far away from Him: perhaps service alone might give a level of satisfaction they're searching for. Instead of looking at what they do, look at how they act, because the way someone lives their life is evidence of their spiritual life. You can tell the level of someone's spirituality by their fruit—the fruit of the Spirit to be exact: "But the fruit of the Spirit is love, joy, peace, long-suffering, kindness, goodness, faithfulness, gentleness, self-control. Against such there is no law" (Gal. 5:22–23).

Is this person peaceful, or are they constantly fighting with others? Do they act out in anger when something doesn't go their way and hold grudges? Are they willing to suffer through afflictions and not turn away from God? Do they treat others kindly and lovingly, not just you? Are they faithful even when no one is watching? Do they demonstrate self-control, or do they lust after their desires? These things take time to discover. Although no one is perfect (and neither are you), emulating the fruit of the Spirit should be a joint goal.

One thing that really attracted me to Fr. Antony was his dedication to Church and ministry. Before we started dating, we had served in a homeless ministry together. On Sunday nights, we would gather with a group of youth at a local church and walk over to an area where many homeless people gathered. We handed out slices of pizza and shared the Gospel with whoever would listen. Many of the homeless people struggled with addictions to alcohol and drugs, and we wanted to find tangible ways to impact their lives other than feeding them on Sunday nights.

I had searched for homelessness assistance programs, rehab houses, and detox programs we could connect them to, and I found a program in the same city where I went to college and a social worker willing to talk to me. No one from the volunteer group was free to come with me to visit the social worker, but Fr. Antony offered to move around some of his commitments to join me. We met with this helpful social worker who patiently answered all our questions and provided us with helpful information to bring back to those we met with on Sunday nights.

I remember driving back from that meeting and telling myself I wanted someone like him. Someone to support me in ministries I cared about and who would go out of his way for me. Little did I know that I'd be the one supporting him years later when he was called to the priesthood. When I remind him of this story, he claims he doesn't remember it, but his actions caught my attention then, and he still continues to amaze me with all that he does for others.

Checking Your Checklist

After reviewing a client's list and challenging them on some characteristics (if needed), I ask them to prioritize the most important qualities and place them at the top. If salvation is the goal of marriage, then you want someone who can help you get there. How big their bank account is, how great they look, or even how they make you feel won't matter as much as how godly they are. I advise that spiritual characteristics should sit at the top of the list. Someone who has Christ at the center of their life will live in a way that aligns with biblical principles.

How do they show up to fight their spiritual battles? How easily do they give up when things aren't going smoothly? How do they prioritize God and the Church? What are the intentions behind their ministry? These are the things you want to examine.

Additionally, each person should possess all the qualities they're looking for in a partner. We attract those who are similar to us, so if you want to meet someone of a certain caliber, you must be able to provide the same level of quality. Evaluate yourself before evaluating others, and know what you can offer in a relationship. You cannot expect to only receive in a relationship; you must also be able to give.

While we must choose carefully who to date, it's possible to be overly picky. If a client finds themselves being too picky about who they are willing to date, I suggest they make another type of list. When they argue that they have all the positive qualities they're looking for on their checklist and can't find anyone that measures up to it, I don't suggest they change their list or lower their standards, but I ask them to make a list of their own flaws. I rarely suggest this, especially not to someone struggling with self-esteem, but if someone is fixated on others' flaws and has a hard time seeing the good in others, then it might be time for a humility check. No one is perfect, and if they can find someone willing to accept them with their flaws (as they work on them), they should be willing to do the same.

Myths about Dating

Myth # 1: I need to date to figure out what I'm looking for.

Trying to figure out what you're looking for while dating is like looking for a road map to your destination after you've hit the road. You will likely get lost and take much longer to arrive at your destination. It is much wiser to have the road map on hand and have previously studied it before starting your journey. Plus, when you're dating, there's another person along for the ride, so your haphazard wandering also affects someone else. You don't want to figure out what you're looking for at the expense of someone else's feelings. So the best way to date is to figure out what you are looking for *before* you start dating. And knowing yourself well is vital to understanding what kind of person would complement your personality. This is where having a good relationship with yourself comes in handy.

You should also know what things are a deal-breaker for you. These are the red flags that you will not tolerate in any relationship. You don't need to experience red flags to know you don't want them present. Figure out what those red flags are for you so that as soon as you experience them, it's your signal to reevaluate the relationship.

This is not to say you won't learn things along the way as you're dating. One positive thing that can come out of relationships that end is understanding what made them not work out. As you have different experiences you might also learn more about what you're like in a relationship and what kind of partner works well with you. Dating might inform your decision to add or remove things from your checklist; just be sure you have one in the first place.

Myth #2: If I don't feel a spark immediately, I'm with the wrong person.

I sometimes hear from clients or friends, "They're a great person, but I'm just not feeling a spark," or something along those lines. As I discussed earlier, people are often looking for the spark, fireworks, or butterfly feelings they imagine they'll feel when they meet "the one." But here's the thing about passionate feelings: You can't trust them to be good relationship indicators. Sparks naturally fizzle out and are not long-lasting. Fireworks eventually hit the ground and disappear. And butterfly feelings can be rooted in anxiety and nervousness.[24] Entertainment outlets have set us up with unrealistic

---

24   Debra Fileta, *True Love Dates: Your Indispensable Guide to Finding the Love of Your Life* (Grand Rapids, MI: Zondervan, 2013), 182–184.

expectations of what it feels like when we meet the love of our life, but no romantic music plays when our love interest walks into the room, as you see portrayed in the movies. Romantic comedies and Disney movies usually depict stories of infatuation and the romantic chase—things that won't set you up for success.

Building a strong connection takes time and holds more value than experiencing instant chemistry. Allow time to pass to see if that connection grows over time. Let logic lead your decision-making process, rather than emotions, which are constantly fluctuating. Your emotions will certainly be present, but they should not be steering the ship when it comes to making important decisions.

Myth #3: I need to find someone who checks every box on my checklist.

No one is perfect, and we are all a work in progress. It's easy to write down all the attributes of your ideal partner. But the chances that someone will check off every box, depending on how long your list is, aren't very high, just like you might not check off someone else's entire checklist. Does this mean you should give up and feel hopeless that no one can meet your expectations? No, this means you should treat potential partners gracefully rather than rigorously. Your list might be perfect, but no human is perfect.

There should be a core group of nonnegotiables on your checklist that you must have in a relationship. The other items can be secondary. And don't confuse the importance of simple things you have in common with the core things you need. For example, you both could have the same taste in food and movies, but those things are not crucial to building a life together. Sure, you'll save a lot of time not having to argue over what to eat for dinner or what movie to watch, but it doesn't hold as much significance as other things, like how you view God.

Ask yourself what qualities you can't live without. For me, I needed someone who pursues God the same way I do. Someone with a forgiving heart because I know how often I make mistakes, and I need someone who will quickly forgive me. Someone reliable, who helps me face all the hardships of life. I wouldn't want someone who was dishonest in his job or studies because a lack of integrity reveals a deeper moral problem. Honesty, integrity, and loyalty were essential characteristics I needed in a husband. What are your non-negotiables? I would rather you stay single than settle for someone who doesn't fit with your nonnegotiables.

4

How to Date

Once you have a clear idea of what kind of person you would want to date, the next thing to figure out is *how* you're going to date. There are endless resources, between online articles, books, and videos, on how you should go about dating. It is important to filter through such content because much of it can contradict your faith and values. Be wise about where and who you get your dating advice from.

Dating with Intention and Clarity

I was sitting at my desk during my senior year summer internship and texting my now husband. We had been good friends up to that point, and he had just graduated from college a month prior. We'd only had a few interactions since then, so I was excited when he reached out. He told me he was planning to attend a youth retreat, and the topic was marriage. I joked about how I didn't think he wanted to get married. After a few lighthearted exchanges, I found him calling me. Little did I know that on the other side of the phone, he was working up the courage to ask me out on a date.

I was still unsure how he wanted to live his life—single in a monastery or married. I only knew he was heading to St. Vladimir's Orthodox Theological Seminary for the next two years for a master's degree in theology. So when he expressed interest in me, I was pleasantly surprised. He laid out his intentions very clearly. He expressed his feelings for me and wanted to see if we could have a future together. I sincerely appreciated his clarity and transparency. I didn't have to guess his intentions or try to read between any lines to figure out how he felt. I obviously said yes, and the rest is history.

There should be no guessing games in mature interactions. Don't listen to popular unwise advice that modern dating tends to preach, such as "Don't text or call back right away; it will make you look desperate," "Date multiple people at once so you don't limit your options," or "Play hard to get, and they'll want you more." No one should be acting a certain way just to manipulate someone's actions, but rather everyone should be honest in their interactions and allow the other to respond accordingly. I also don't recommend dating several people at once; that often leads to confusion. It is better to talk to one person at a time to evaluate if they're what you're looking for rather than comparing them with multiple people.

If you like someone, tell them. If you're no longer interested, also tell them. If you're someone who will drop everything to respond to calls and messages right away, tell the other person what to expect. If you typically don't promptly respond to messages or calls, give them a heads-up. Establish clear expectations around communication from the start. No one is a mind reader, and if you are ever confused, ask for clarity. Clear communication is vital to the beginning and continuation of every relationship.

Ghosting someone, meaning you stop responding to them without an explanation, is an impolite and immature way of ending dating interactions or a relationship. You might not be ready to date if you're not mature enough to bring closure to a dating relationship. If someone has been extensively talking with you or took the time to go out with you on one or several dates, you owe it to them to officially part ways. A simple explanation can go a long way, for example, "I appreciate your time and enjoyed getting to know you, but I don't think we're a good fit for each other." If your interactions consist of virtual communication, then saying goodbye virtually is acceptable, but if you have gone on many dates, it might not be appropriate to break up in a text message. Although you might fear hurting their feelings, leaving someone guessing as to what happened is no better. Everyone risks getting hurt feelings when they set out to date, knowing that not every interaction or relationship will end in their favor. But all must be willing to take that risk if they plan to date.

A Word to Men

Loving men, I want to see you lead with clarity and eliminate confusion. If you're afraid of putting yourself out there, you might find yourself trying to play it safe by being vague, fearing rejection. Sometimes your lack of clarity comes from a place of insecurity, and it leaves the woman guessing about your intentions and interest. I want you to face those insecurities and lead with confidence, knowing you have a lot to offer.

If you are interested in a friend romantically, the easiest way to explore that romantic interest is through a date (a.k.a. moving out of the friend zone). Instead, it may be tempting to seek a bulletproof plan to guarantee she'll say yes rather than risk rejection. Rejection isn't easy, but you have to take the risk if you think the reward is worth it. If you are rejected, try to look at the rejection in a positive light as a way of knowing this person wasn't the one for you, and now you're one step closer to finding your person.

Even if you feel intimidated by the idea of approaching women, the more you do it, the more comfortable you'll become. Interact in a kind and loving way, and you'll be surprised at the positive reaction from women. Don't let one or two bad interactions deter you from putting yourself out there. Some women are waiting for you to make the first move. They want you to pursue them and make them feel they are worth your time and effort. And some women will even make it easier for you by going out of their way to show interest. Pick up on their cues and take the next step! It helps to have a plan for how you want to get to know her and where you're comfortable meeting. For example, if initial face-to-face coffee or dinner dates feel more like interviews to you, you might want to opt for shoulder-to-shoulder dates where you're doing a fun activity together and discovering each other's personalities.

And keep in mind that you are made in the image of God, according to His likeness, called to love your wife as God loved the Church and died for her. Asking a girl out isn't death, but it's certainly dying to your fear, pride, or any insecurity you might have around rejection. Courage doesn't show up by accident; it grows as you face your fears. So even if starting a relationship or committing to one is scary, do it scared, and your confidence will grow over time. Also, don't take every rejection personally and allow it to knock down your self-esteem. It may be that the girl isn't ready to date or may have had her eye on someone else before you even entered the picture. Or it might be as simple as she doesn't believe you two are a good match and already has her mind made up (whether that's accurate or not).

As you date a woman, continually communicate with her what's on your mind. Tell her you want to date her exclusively if that's what you decide and how serious you feel about her. Check in with each other periodically to make sure you're on the same page. And if one of you is on a different page or has unreciprocated feelings, then politely go your separate ways. Again, don't take this personally, as the goal of dating is to determine if you're right for each other.

A Word to Women

Kind ladies, I know you're eager to be in the relationship you've always dreamed of. Some of you may even feel like your clock is ticking and you want to become a wife and mother, knowing there might be a deadline to the latter. Trusting in God's timing and being patient can be quite challenging. You might be meeting men you'd like to get to know romantically and growing tired of waiting for them to approach you. You can certainly approach them first, or there are some things you can do to encourage them to take the first step.

What you can do is drop some hints that you are interested in him. Go out of your way to start a conversation, and remember important details he shares with you. Ask him about himself and show him you're listening to make him feel seen. If you have already dropped hints, it might be that he's completely unaware of them, or perhaps he's not interested, or he's still afraid to ask you out. Hopefully, it's not the first (assuming that you've made your hints clear). If it's the second and he's not interested, that's okay, and it's your signal to move on. If he's still worried about asking you out, then he most likely likes to play it safe and is afraid to take a risk, which might be a recurring theme in his life. Then you have to ask yourself if you're okay with that characteristic. Or, sometimes the man will take longer to come to terms with his feelings and make a move, so be patient and give him some time. He might not move as fast as you, and that's okay.

If a guy does ask you out and you're not interested, kindly be clear and honest with him. Communicate in a way that shows appreciation for his efforts while you don't share his interest. Don't give the false impression that there might still be a chance in the future if you know that there isn't. And keep your interactions confidential between you two. You don't want to be the girl who tells everyone about her dating life, and no man wants his rejection to be public knowledge. It will hurt him and make him hesitant with the next girl he meets. Look out for your community of sisters by treating your brothers with love and respect.

If you find yourself in a situation where you're unclear about the man's intention, and he has not made it clear, have the courage to ask him. If things are vague, you don't need to wait passively, afraid you might scare him off. If you're acting like a couple but have not officially committed to one another, it's time to eliminate the ambiguity and initiate a conversation around defining the relationship.

Online Dating

While I prefer people to meet in person, I cannot ignore the realities of online dating. According to research done in 2019 and 2022 by the Pew Research Center, "Three-in-ten U.S. adults say they have ever used a dating site or app."[25] More people are meeting online

---

25 Colleen McClain and Risa Gelles-Watnick, "From Looking for Love to Swiping the Field: Online Dating in the U.S.," Pew Research Center, February 2, 2023, https://www.pewresearch.org/internet/2023/02/02 /from-looking-for-love-to-swiping-the-field-online-dating-in-the-u-s/.

these days, and there is no denying their success stories. In successful relationships, it doesn't matter how you meet, but how you date.

If you want to try to meet someone without using a dating app, I first encourage you to get involved in your local church community and serve alongside other God-loving people your age. You can also step out of your comfort zone and attend faith-based functions, events, or national conferences that will allow you to meet other Christian singles. Also, don't overlook telling your trusted circle of friends or family that you are open to being set up if they know someone they think would be a good match for you. It's great to have someone who knows your character and can vouch for someone else they think you'd be compatible with.

But suppose you don't have the privilege of meeting people in those ways and you find yourself in a small church community or a geographical location that lacks many Christian singles. In that case, online dating might be an excellent tool for you. But remember that not all dating apps are the same. Do your research to see what app is most suitable for you and what you're looking for. I always recommend using Christian dating apps (there are even some Orthodox ones), or at least using the Christian filters on regular dating apps.

Some apps limit the number of matches you can see per day, and some allow endless swiping. Be wary of those apps that have a plethora of options, because as research has found, more choices lead to greater dissatisfaction. A study that examined analysis paralysis (the act of overthinking or overanalyzing a situation, which leads to not being able to make a decision) in customers found that when customers had more choices they bought less. When people are bombarded with too many choices, they are overwhelmed by the number of variables they have to consider and are left crippled (or paralyzed) and can't make a decision.[26] Don't let this be the case in online dating. If your dating app doesn't limit the number of profiles you can see at once, I suggest setting your own limit so you are not facing your own analysis paralysis.

When looking for the right relationship, searching for perfection will leave you empty-handed; instead, be realistic about the kind of relationship that will satisfy you. In the book *Paradox of Choice*, the author distinguishes between two kinds of people: satisficers and maximizers.[27] Satisficers are content with an adequate solution that meets their criteria, while maximizers only want the best solution and must compare all possible solutions before picking the right one. When it comes to dating, satisficers are happy once they meet someone who fits the criteria they want. On the other hand, a maximizer needs to make sure the person they're with is the best possible choice. They can exhaust themselves looking for something better, and during that process they may pass up many people who are good enough. They may also get caught in an endless loop of comparing people. Research shows that maximizers experience more anxiety and regret and less happiness with decisions they make.

So make sure you are realistic with the criteria you set, and be satisfied when you find it in a person. Don't get trapped in trying to see what else is out there, whether online or in person. The best way to approach meeting people online is the same way you'd approach meeting in person: stick to your purpose, be intentional, communicate with clarity, know what you're looking for, and most importantly, be open-minded—especially when it comes to people's looks.

---

26   Rony Kurien, Anil Rao Paila, and Asha Nagendra, "Application of Paralysis Analysis Syndrome in Customer Decision Making," *Procedia Economics and Finance* 11 (January 2014): 323–34, https://doi.org/10.1016/s2212-5671 (14)00200-7.

27   Barry Schwartz, *The Paradox of Choice: Why More is Less* (New York, NY: HarperCollins, 2004), 81–87.

You know that rule you were taught about not judging a book by its cover? Well, online dating is a great time to apply this. It's easy to sit in the comfort of your home, scrolling through hundreds of different profiles and only swiping on the ones that immediately catch your attention. But how you evaluate a potential partner has to be more extensive than that—partly because, whether you realize it or not (and whether you like it or not), the media has influenced your standards of beauty. One study has demonstrated this issue with its research on the role mass media has on the increase of body surveillance, which is the act of constantly assessing one's external appearance with that of culturally valued ideals. Not only did this study find that body surveillance has negative psychological outcomes on individuals, but constant analysis of a romantic partner's body was associated with lower relationship satisfaction.[28] This proves that the more you compare your body or your partner's body to the beauty standard influenced by mass media, the less satisfied you become in your romantic relationships.

Most people you meet aren't the supermodel type you've dreamed about (and most likely, you aren't either). So don't judge someone from a few pictures and make a hasty decision just on that. Consider the information they share about themselves on the app and see what you have in common. See how they communicate with you and whether you can start and keep a good conversation going with them.

Also, as you are getting to know someone, whether online or in person, make sure you don't fall into the trap of falling in love with who you *think* they are. You might be tempted to jump to conclusions based on a few facts that you know. For example, you see a

---

28   Chiara Rollero, "Mass Media Beauty Standards, Body Surveillance, and Relationship Satisfaction within Romantic Couples," *International Journal of Environmental Research and Public Health* 19, no. 7 (March 2022): 3833, https://doi.org/10.3390/ijerph19073833.

picture of them participating in a sport and assume they're adventurous and athletic. You know they hold a prestigious job, so you assume they're hardworking and highly ambitious. Or you see them in a picture with a group of people and assume they're great at keeping friends. While all those assumptions might be true, in reality, it could be that they rarely play sports, they're barely just getting by at work, and those friend gatherings are a rare occurrence. Additionally, when you start romanticizing who someone is, you create expectations they can't meet. Your expectations can tend to err on the side of perfection, as you want to imagine yourself with the best possible partner and overlook their flaws and imperfections. But in reality, everyone is humanly imperfect, and creating unrealistic expectations will not set you up for success.

I want you to learn to see things at face value until you learn more about a person. Figure out the right questions to ask to discover their personality. Allow yourself to get to know them slowly and steadily, and allow them to get to know you as well. Don't build false expectations by dreaming about a future with someone you just met or before committing to a serious relationship. This might leave you grieving a relationship that never really existed. Ensure you have the proper boundaries to keep you from jumping in too deep too quickly.

Setting Your Dating Boundaries

While you might be excited to jump into the dating pool immediately—in person or online—don't forget to set your dating boundaries first and honor them as you go. And I'm not just talking about physical boundaries but emotional ones as well.

Physical intimacy is powerful, and exercising it at the wrong time can negatively affect the relationship and those involved.

God designed sex for the marriage covenant (more on this in chapter 8), and anything outside of that strips away its holiness and sanctity, but not necessarily its biological effects. Research shows that sexual arousal actually deactivates a region in the frontal cortex of the brain. And since the frontal cortex is responsible for critical thinking, rational behavior, and self-awareness, this deactivation makes it hard for you to make rational decisions when you're sexually intimate.[29] In other words, when you're sexually aroused, you're not thinking straight. This means that a sexual connection with someone might keep you stuck in a relationship that isn't good for you because it clouds your judgment and makes all the red flags undetectable. Or you might know it's the wrong relationship for you, but the temptation to stay becomes stronger than your desire to leave.

We know that the Bible clearly states that fornication (sex before marriage) is a sin, but physical boundaries aren't just for abstaining from sex; they're for guarding your purity. So you will need to figure out where to draw your line so that you're not leading your body into sexual temptation. This line differs for everyone, and where you draw the line might even vary according to which person you're dating (if their limits are more conservative). In general, I suggest staying away from anything that leads to sexual arousal because once your body is there, it gets much harder to practice self-control, since your frontal cortex is not fully activated. For some, it could be kissing, and for some, it could be a touch even less intimate than that. Generally, if it's something you wouldn't do in public with your partner, don't do it in private. And avoid being

---

29   Semir Zeki, "The Neurobiology of Love," *FEBS Letters* 581, no. 14 (June 2007): 2575–79, https://doi.org/10.1016/j.febslet.2007.03.094.

in private settings with no one around, where accountability is low, and temptation is high.

As your relationship progresses, you should have discussions about sexual boundaries, and it is imperative that you agree on what those boundaries are and what type of affection you are comfortable with. Keeping those boundaries might be a struggle, but you need them nonetheless. Make sure to take into account the other person's feelings; a relationship isn't just about you and guarding your purity but also about your partner's. And if you find yourself in a relationship where the other person isn't respecting your boundaries, that could be a red flag. If you find your partner's lack of self-control threating your purity, then it might be time to reevaluate the relationship.

. . . . .

Emotional intimacy is also important in a relationship and must be built with caution and guarded with the proper boundaries, as Proverbs 4:23 says, "Keep your heart with all diligence, / For out of it *spring* the issues of life." Sharing your innermost thoughts and feelings with someone has to be done wisely and with discretion, since being open and vulnerable builds a bond between two people.

The more someone earns your trust, the more you can share about yourself and open up to them. So don't spill everything on the first date; take it slow and steadily build your emotional connection. The beginning of a relationship should be about exploring if you're a good match for each other and finding out about the person's personality and lifestyle. You might miss many important things if you dive into the deep end immediately; instead, start in the shallow end and make your way deeper at the right pace. Debra Fileta, a licensed professional counselor and relationship expert, warns, "Don't go too deep too fast, because emotional intimacy can pull you far deeper into your relationship than you ever meant to go and, in the end, leave you with the double damage of a broken heart and broken spirit."[30]

When you share private things about your past that can affect the future of your current relationship, make sure the other person has gotten to know who you are in the present so they're not only seeing you through the light of your past. No one is free from sin; hopefully, we're all making progress and have come a long way. Your past does not define you, nor should your partner judge who you are today based on it. Also, you want to be sure that this person will be an honest keeper of the information you trust them with.

In addition to sharing any previous relationship history, you might need to share about a mental or physical health condition. Shared at the right time, it can help your partner understand you more. By then they won't be looking to label you, but it will provide them with a better picture of who you are and how they can better meet your needs.

· · · · ·

Another critical element to put a boundary around is your time: having parameters on how much time and when you spend time with someone will help guard your physical and emotional boundaries. For example, if you find a peak in sexual temptation after a particular hour of the night or after being with each other for an extensive amount of time, limit the time you spend together.

Additionally, while it's natural to want to spend all your time with someone you're building a connection with, it's not always healthy. Having independence and spending time apart is beneficial

---

30 Fileta, *True Love Dates: Your Indispensable Guide to Finding the Love of Your Life*, 99.

so that you don't find yourself in an overly dependent relationship. Don't get swept up in a romantic partnership and neglect time for yourself and other meaningful relationships. You still need time to get to know and develop yourself, and to meet your needs that may be beyond the scope of the relationship. And if a relationship ends, your friends and family will still be there for you if you've maintained a connection with them, so don't sever your bond with them for the sake of being in a relationship. There should be a balance between the time you spend with your romantic partner and your friends and family so that they can harmoniously coexist in your life.

Also, if you have not committed to a serious relationship with someone, you should limit the amount of time and kind of interactions you have. Someone in the friend category should not receive the same attention, time, and commitment as someone you're dating. If you spend a lot of one-on-one time with someone of the opposite sex and constantly talk to them, it might be a sign that this person means more to you than just a friend, and it might be time to act on it. And if the feelings aren't mutual, it's better to know right away rather than to keep investing emotionally, hoping for a different outcome. Guard your heart by putting the right boundaries in place.

Myths about How to Date

Myth #1: I need to be sure this is the right person before I start dating them.

When we put a lot of pressure on a date, we believe this myth. While it helps to do your homework first and get to know as much as you can about someone before you go on a date with them, it's not always practical. In any case, the entire point of dating is to determine if they are suitable for you. If you have the privilege of getting to know them as a friend first, that's great; but if you cannot, then a date—or a few dates—is the right setting in which to do so. It might help to have a few phone calls or video chats before meeting in person. That way, you can assess if there is a chance of compatibility before going out on a date. Getting to know each other a bit first might save you both time, effort, and money.

If dating generally feels like too much pressure, then it might be a sign you need to take some of that pressure off yourself. This mentality can sometimes stem from thinking that dating must lead to marriage—and while ultimately you hope it does—you don't know with whom. So take it one date at a time. The goal of the first date shouldn't be to see if you want to marry the person; it should be gauging if you like them enough to want a second date. Each date should lead to the next if there is mutual interest. Know what qualities you're looking for, and see if they possess those qualities as you go along.

Myth #2: Online dating is for those who are desperate.

Not everyone is privileged to live in an area with many dating prospects. And even then, not everyone is great at meeting new people. There is no shame in meeting people through the convenience of modern technology. The more we repeat this myth, the more stigma we create around online dating and discourage others from using it for good. Online dating is no more than a different way to meet someone new; or at the very least, it will make you aware of people you already know who are looking to start a relationship.

You might even convince yourself there's no point in online dating because you don't believe it can work. This thought only becomes true if you keep repeating it to yourself and it becomes a self-fulfilling prophecy. It's fine to decide that online dating isn't for you and that you only want to meet people in person. But if you're going to give it a try, don't go in with a negative mentality. I know many couples who have met online and have gotten married, and you probably do too.

Myth #3: I'll figure out my dating boundaries as I go.

Doing as much prep work as possible will help you in the long run. Don't wait until you're in the heat of the moment with someone you find very attractive to figure out what boundaries you're comfortable with. Chances are, by that point you'll have little self-control and may not be able to instill any boundaries at all. Also, know your emotional boundaries before you find yourself regretting something you share. Know what level of trust you're looking for in order to feel comfortable sharing certain things about yourself.

Not only is it essential to know what your physical and emotional boundaries are, but it's important to communicate them to the person you're dating. You both should be on the same page or at least feel comfortable honoring each other's boundaries. Your boundaries can say a lot about your values, which is another indicator of compatibility. So if you haven't yet figured out what your boundaries are, the time to do so is now, even before you begin dating.

5

Check for Compatibility

On my first Valentine's Day with Fr. Antony, I woke up to a beautiful sunny morning with a brisk February breeze, excited about the day. He had just proposed a few weeks prior, and I was wondering what great plans he had for us that day (I eventually found out that he was not the planning type but the spur-of-the-moment type). So I was surprised to find him calling me that morning, telling me his priest had asked if he could drive him to Philadelphia for a campus ministry that night. It would be about a three-hour drive round trip from where we lived. I thought he would cancel our date, but then he asked if I would join him and I said yes.

That year we had agreed that making gifts would be more meaningful than buying them (we were also students on a budget, so it was a great idea). I spent all day painting him his favorite Psalm on a canvas, skipping lunch so I wouldn't miss our evening appointment. After driving the priest to his destination and attending part of his speaking engagement, we found ourselves in a quiet part of an unfamiliar town. By then, I was starving and couldn't wait to eat, so we got directions to the nearest restaurant within walking distance, which was a local pizzeria. The pizzeria turned out to be a liquor store with a few rundown seats—not the most romantic location for a first Valentine's Day date. It was a cash-only place, and we mainly carried credit cards, but we managed to scrape together enough change for two slices of pizza.

We exchanged a few awkward glances at the homeless people sitting in the booth across from us, then looked at each other and laughed at where we had ended up—a place much different than what I had imagined when I woke up that day. But that ended up being the most memorable Valentine's Day to date. No fancy restaurant or extravagant gift has topped that in the years that followed. It was a day filled with sweet encounters, fruitful conversations, and meaningful service. It was simple, yet it connected us to each other and to the things we cared about, like serving others.

Our relationship wasn't just about ourselves; it was always greater than just the two of us. It was about our love for God and going wherever He called us, whether to Philly for campus ministry or to Australia indefinitely (we almost moved to Australia after our first year of marriage, but that's a story for another time). Our compatibility stemmed from finding joy in similar things, one of which was service.

The Five Fs of Compatibility

After you've figured out what you're looking for in a partner, next comes checking for compatibility once you've entered into a relationship. Compatibility is not just about the things you have in common with someone, because you can have a lot in common but have a terrible time getting along. Rather, your ability to relate, connect, and share the same views and values makes for excellent compatibility. Keep in mind that perfect compatibility doesn't exist because no two people are exactly the same. We are all shaped by different experiences, resulting in unique personalities that make for beautiful relationships.

There are several areas to consider when evaluating compatibility between two people, and I believe there are five main categories of compatibility. These five "F" categories can make or break a relationship: faith is the core value, and the other four are fighting, family/friends, fun, and future.

Diagram 2: The Five Fs of Compatibility

Faith

One of my favorite high school teachers was a proud atheist. I loved his English literature classes because he ran them like college philosophy classes where debate was always welcomed. His way of teaching opened my mind to different worlds and ways of thinking, and reaffirmed everything I believed about mine. Although my faith and his lack of faith couldn't have been further apart, I was delighted to be challenged by him.

One day as we were discussing intercultural and interfaith marriages, I spoke about how faith was an important thing to have in common with a partner. He asked me, "Well, what if you meet someone with a different faith background that you're attracted to?" I simply answered, "Then I probably wouldn't want him." I'm not sure how much I knew about the kind of person I wanted to marry when I was in high school (my silly list probably included criteria like having a six-pack, soft hair, and being an avid swimmer), but I knew enough to know that faith was a nonnegotiable.

The way we view God and practice our faith builds the foundational truths that govern our lives, and our beliefs shape our identity and influence our actions from trivial to significant ways. Our faith trickles into how we live, express our deepest concerns, and face our most challenging struggles. Because of this, faith influences every other category of compatibility. It influences how you respect and love your partner, the way you honor your father and mother, how you esteem your friends, your choice of fun activities, how you handle your finances, what you believe about gender roles, and much more. It also influences your political stance and your views on societal issues, and how you feel about the role of God or the role of the state in relation to them. Faith acts as a guide on these essential matters and is the road map to navigating all of life.

Faith becomes a major roadblock if you and your partner are not on the same page regarding spiritual beliefs. And even if you are of the same faith, the way you practice your faith can vary. Some make faith the focal point of their life, and some place it off to the side and only tend to it occasionally. You should agree on what you believe and how you practice it, not just for yourselves but also for the children you might have in the future. Spiritual beliefs are the cornerstone of a steady marriage and the backbone of a strong family. Indeed, in a marriage, religious agreement helps prevent problems, resolve conflict, and reconcile the relationship.[31]

Fighting

It may sound strange to include fighting as a part of compatibility, but the ability to fight well is essential because arguments, disagreements, and quarreling are inevitable in every relationship. Drs. John and Julie Gottman, world-renowned relationship researchers and psychologists, state that there are two types of fights couples face: solvable and perpetual.[32] Solvable fights have solutions: these types of problems are often logistical and a compromise can be reached. Perpetual problems are deeply rooted in differences in personalities, priorities, values, and beliefs. These problems will keep reoccurring; in fact, they make up 69 percent of the problems in relationships. So it's good to keep in mind that if you find yourself in a dating relationship that has numerous perpetual problems, this could be a sign of a fundamental incompatibility. Hence the more compatible you are, the less you will face perpetual problems in your relationship (even though some problems will still exist).

The Gottman's book *Fight Right*, although not a faith-based marriage book, addresses exactly how to turn conflict into connection. Additionally, it also mentions that the way a couple communicates

31 Nathaniel M. Lambert and David C. Dollahite, "How Religiosity Helps Couples Prevent, Resolve, and Overcome Marital Conflict," *Family Relations: An Interdisciplinary Journal of Applied Family Studies* 55, no. 4 (September 2006): 439–449, https://doi.org/10.1111/j.1741-3729.2006.00413.x.

32 Julie Schwartz Gottman and John Gottman, *Fight Right: How Successful Couples Turn Conflict Into Connection* (New York, NY: Harmony, 2024), 15.

about problems, even the ones without a clear solution, will either build connection between them or drive them apart. One way healthy conflict management brings couples closer is that it allows them to understand one another by listening to each other's feelings and ideas behind an argument. The Gottmans point out how neuropsychological research shows that problem-solving involves both logical thinking and emotions.[33] And with each fight the couple can learn more about one other and how they process the world around them; this allows for moments of connection.

* * * * *

Communicating well and resolving conflicts are foundational to a healthy relationship, and a couple's ability to share their feelings, understand each other, and listen to one another is essential for moving through life together in a positive way. Good relationships are based on trust, and opening up about your true feelings is an important part of building that trust. The more you feel like your partner is *listening* to you, not just *hearing* you, the more you are likely to open up and share positive and negative feelings. Your partner's reaction or response will make a difference regarding how vulnerable you're willing to be in your communication.

Coming from different families of origin, you might be accustomed to certain ways of communicating, and bringing that into a relationship can be a source of tension. Grace and Lucas found themselves in this predicament. Lucas grew up in a family where emotions were kept at bay and not discussed. He came from a hardworking immigrant family whose main goal was survival, where making it through hard days was physically exhausting and left no energy for emotional discussions at the end of the night. Whenever

---

33 Gottman and Gottman, 108.

Lucas tried to bring up something with his parents that he was unhappy about, they usually brushed him off and told him to be grateful for what he had. Lucas wasn't being ungrateful by wanting to express his feelings about certain situations, but after multiple failed attempts to communicate with his parents, he began to suppress his feelings and keep his thoughts to himself.

Conversely, Grace was outspoken and had no issues with communicating what was on her mind. She grew up in a home where family meetings were a reoccurring habit, and her family spoke about any and everything, sweeping nothing under the rug. From a young age, she was encouraged to express her feelings. Grace's parents were open to hearing her concerns and answering her questions, which made her confident in speaking up.

When Grace and Lucas were dating, it was no surprise that they had difficulty communicating. They had no issues with feeling connected when things were going well, but when things got difficult, they seemed to hit a wall. Grace didn't have trouble talking and sharing how she felt, and whenever they faced a problem, she wanted to dissect it until they found a solution. However, Lucas would avoid discussing negative situations that made him uncomfortable. Their different ways of resolving conflict drove them apart rather than brought them closer together, but with the help of coaching and by learning active listening techniques they were on their way to improving their communication, and ultimately their relationship.

Conflict will naturally arise in every relationship, and a couple's ability to discuss and resolve differences says a lot about the health of their relationship. If there are no conflicts in a relationship, chances are they are being avoided—which causes more harm than good because suppressed feelings will always bubble to the surface, and usually not in the best way. The other extreme is being stuck in a never-ending cycle of conflict, which might indicate a lack of compatibility or poor communication and conflict resolution skills. Both cases are an indication that something isn't right in the relationship.

According to the Thomas-Kilmann Conflict Mode Instrument, there are five different conflict resolution styles: avoiding, accommodating, competing, compromising, and collaborating.[34] These styles are also measured on a scale of assertiveness and cooperativeness. While people tend to lean toward one of these styles, you might use all of them in different situations (i.e., at work, at home, with friends).

In the avoiding style, the person doesn't address any issues, nor do they want to deal with any conflict. Never addressing their concern avoids any confrontation they might have to face. Avoiders are uncooperative and unassertive, a combination that doesn't work well in relationships. We can safely assume that Lucas leaned more toward this conflict resolution style.

Accommodating people tend to overlook their own concerns and instead focus on satisfying the other person. If they do this too often without a similar exchange from their partner, it becomes an unhealthy form of self-sacrifice. Complying with the other person's wishes and neglecting your needs will result in a one-sided relationship. While this is a cooperative style, it can build resentment over time if your needs are never addressed or met. It also ranks low on the assertive scale, as you do not voice your needs.

---

34   Kenneth Thomas and Ralph Kilmann, "Take the Thomas-Kilmann Conflict Mode Instrument (TKI)," *Kilmann Diagnostics,* accessed December 12, 2022, https://kilmanndiagnostics.com/overview-thomas-kilmann-conflict-mode-instrument-tki/.

Competing is the opposite of accommodating. Here, a person is assertive and strong-willed, and they know what they want and how to get it. They will use their power to win, and they believe that their way is the only way. This might keep them from being sensitive to the desires and needs of others, especially their partner.

Compromising people tend to view resolutions as 50/50. They give a little and take a little in order to meet in the middle. They aim to find a mutually acceptable solution that satisfies both parties as much as possible, and finding a happy middle ground is their way of resolving conflict. Compromisers land right in the middle of the scale of assertiveness and cooperativeness, as they tend to be balanced in both.

Collaborating goes one step further than compromising: it is highly assertive and cooperative. Collaborators want to find a solution where everyone wins; they want to get to the root cause of the problem and address the disagreement in depth. Grace would identify with the collaborating style, the opposite of the avoiding style. Hence, she and Lucas never saw eye to eye and struggled to resolve their conflicts.

It's helpful to know which conflict resolution style you tend to use, as well as your partner's. You might find yourself on opposite sides of the conflict resolution spectrum with your partner, like Grace and Lucas, or you might have similar styles. Over time, you can work on adopting a healthier style if you tend to resort to avoiding, competing, or even accommodating techniques. That was something I had to work on in my relationship.

During our engagement, deep in wedding planning, my then-fiancé and I found ourselves in a heated argument. I was in charge of designing and ordering our wedding invitations. After an extensive search, I found ones that fit our style and budget. I typed out all the details, quickly glanced over them for accuracy, and then purchased nearly two hundred. Days later, when they arrived, we noticed I had missed an important detail: the year of the wedding date. I had the month and day correct but somehow had forgotten the year (a true face-palm moment).

Father Antony insisted on reprinting the cards. I argued that it would be a waste of money and that everyone would know the invites were for this year (because clearly, I thought, no one sends wedding invitations a year early). "I'm not reprinting them. That would be a waste of money. No, I'm not doing it!" I shouted. I then proceeded to leave the room and wanted to make my way out of the house completely. But he gently held me and said, "You can't just leave when something doesn't go your way." And he was right. I wanted to walk away and avoid the problem and maybe deal with it later—not the smartest move. We ended up compromising and only printing half the amount of invitations we had originally ordered and using those invites for our close friends and family. From that day, we set a boundary around resolving conflicts: we could not leave the room in anger; we had to stay and face the problem.

Every couple should have their own set of rules and boundaries for peaceably fighting. Here are a few I recommend: shouting and screaming should be avoided. No name-calling or cursing should take place. Don't leave the house and run away from the argument. It's okay to take a break from an argument and resume it when both parties have calmed down. If you have children in the future, no contentious fighting in front of them (small arguments carried out respectfully are okay, but save the intense discussions for when they're not around). And if you are going to argue in front of the kids make sure they see you resolve it; it's a good way to model healthy conflict resolution. And it goes without saying: absolutely no physical harm to each other.

Family/Friends

Whenever someone says, "I'm marrying this person, not the family," I chuckle a little. The truth is, you are marrying their family as well because family—and friends, too—play a significant role in relationships. When you sign up to be with someone, you are also signing up to be a part of their family and friend groups. It is important to understand your partner's family dynamics and how they will be involved in your joint life going forward. It is also helpful to use the time of dating and engagement for both families to get acquainted with each other. Their ability or inability to get along will give you a glimpse into how they will interact in the future after you are married.

Also, getting to know your partner's group of friends will help you get to know your partner better. The activities they participate in together and the values they uphold can say a lot about what is important to your partner. It also helps to understand how you both prioritize friendships and how you plan to maintain them after marriage. Finding a healthy balance in the time you spend together and apart can require some work to navigate, but it's important to have both if you want the relationship to thrive.

Friends and family can support your relationship, or they can be problematic. Discuss how you will set up healthy boundaries with each other's friends and family. You should be comfortable with how much influence family and friends will have on your relationship. Your partner's family can be the extended family you've always wanted, or they can be the most challenging part of your relationship. I hope you find that it's the former, but you must be willing to carry that cross if it's the latter.

If your families come from different cultural, ethnic, or racial backgrounds, there will be an added level of complexity that you will need to navigate. According to Dugan Romano, author of

Intercultural Marriage: Promises and Pitfalls, there are nineteen areas that intercultural couples continually cite as trouble spots,[35] some of which are values, sex, male-female roles, politics, finances, social class, religion, raising children, language and communication, and coping with death or divorce. This is not to say that couples from the same culture will not have issues in these areas, but that they are commonly found in intercultural marriages.

It is absolutely possible to find compatibility if you and your partner have different cultural backgrounds; it will just require more work than if you are of the same background. Understanding different heritages, traditions, and customs will require more effort than if they were the same as your own. (The same goes for different socioeconomic backgrounds; it will be a difference you will observe and intentionally have to address.) Reverend Dr. Pishoy Salama, who ministers to many intercultural marriages in his parish in Toronto, Canada, writes in his Doctorate of Ministry dissertation that "evidence has shown that intercultural marriages have their own unique challenges which each couple must face . . . but with love, understanding, and perseverance, these challenges can also be conquered."[36] He reaffirms that those of different cultural backgrounds can find harmony in their marriages.

Fun

Having fun together as a couple is a vital part of a healthy relationship. Finding pleasure in the same activities will allow you and

---

35   Dugan Romano, *Intercultural Marriage: Promises and Pitfalls*, e-book ed. (Boston, MA: Nicholas Brealey, 2008), 63.

36   Fr. Pishoy Salama, "Of All Nations: Exploring Intercultural Marriages in the Coptic Orthodox Church of the GTA" (DMin diss., Toronto School of Theology, 2012), 61, https://hdl.handle.net/1807/34898.

your partner to bond over shared interests. There will also be fewer disagreements and indecisions about what to do together, and quality time will be easier to plan—though having fun together is not just about enjoying the same activities but about your ability to get along and enjoy each other's company.

Making fun a priority means committing to dating your partner for the rest of your life, even after you're married. Devote time to continue getting to know them and giving them your undivided attention. Research has shown that engaging in fun experiences as a couple releases dopamine and norepinephrine, which activates the brain's reward system. These are the same chemicals that are released during early dating, and they can still be produced during marriage when a couple prioritizes having fun together. Some experiments have revealed that couples who go on fun date nights or participate in fun activities have higher relationship satisfaction.[37]

Spending quality, enjoyable time together will grow your relationship, so be clear on the kind and amount of time you want to spend together. Remember though, that you don't have to do *everything* together; it's healthy to set aside time for yourself, for your interests, hobbies, and friends. Being with someone should not consume your life and force you to put the things you care about on the back burner. You should allow each other to pursue your own interests and respect the time you need apart.

Other things that impact a couple's ability to enjoy each other's company are the similarities and differences in their personalities. Although my husband and I have many things in common, we have different personalities. He's an extrovert, preferring to be around people, and I'm an introvert who deeply values being home

---

37   Hannah Eaton, "Choose a Partner You Can Be Playful With," The Gottman, Institute, December 19, 2017, https://www.gottman.com/blog/choose -partner-can-playful/.

alone. He likes to go with the flow, and I want to plan every detail of my life. He has no problem waking up early to seize the day, and you have to drag me out of bed in the morning. He has run marathons, and I can hardly enjoy a light jog. Having different personalities and habits causes tension in our marriage, but these habits also help us to understand each other more deeply and learn how to compromise—and thus, learn how to love each other better.

It took many years to figure out how to balance our differences instead of always ending up in a fight (and there are things we're still working on). For example, we would sometimes argue about how to spend our time, since he prefers going to events, and I often prefer not to. So after we figured out when we would spend quality time together, he would go to some events alone while I stayed home—a solution that makes us both happy and allows us each to have fun in our own way as well as together.

* * * * *

As you date, it's important to become familiar with your partner's personality characteristics, qualities, and habits, since these can either complement yours in a relationship or clash. While there will always be some clashes, you should be overall comfortable and content with your partner's personality traits. For instance, if your partner has a bad temper, demonstrates embarrassing behavior around others, or can be excessively moody, you must be able to accept these negative behaviors if you choose to move forward in the relationship. If they have too many qualities you cannot live with, and you rarely have fun together, the lack of compatibility might bring down the relationship. While you'd like to see your partner in the best light, accepting them at their worst is just as important, so remember that you cannot change someone's personality. Don't marry someone with potential, hoping they will improve over time.

Accept them as they are, and if it's not possible for you to enjoy their company, it's probably time to go your separate ways.

Future

It's a beautiful thing when a couple dreams about their future together because a healthy marriage will help you achieve your goals. You and your partner will become each other's support and cheerleaders as you pursue your individual ambitions and your ambitions as a couple. Being in agreement on how you envision the future will set you on the right track, so it's important as the dating relationship progresses toward engagement that you discuss your ideas around future family lifestyle, financial management, gender roles, and more.

· · · · ·

When our great-grandparents (and maybe grandparents) were raising families, it was more clear cut as to who would be the breadwinner and who would be the homemaker. Men were expected to work hard and solely financially support their family, while women took care of the children and all household duties. This is not often the case today. In fact, in 2022 there were more women in the US labor force than men ages twenty-five and older with a bachelor's degree or more (50.7 percent to be exact), according to a Pew Research Center analysis of government data.[38] Today, both men and women are encouraged to pursue higher education and chase the career of their dreams—so it's especially important to start discussing your expectations around family lifestyle once your relationship starts getting serious.

---

38   "Women Now Outnumber Men in the U.S. College-Educated Labor Force," Pew Research Center, September 22, 2022, https://www.pew research.org/short-reads/2022/09/26/women-now-outnumber-men-in-the -u-s-college-educated-labor-force/.

It is common now for both spouses to financially support their household. But that might not be the desire of every couple. Some women (or some men, though this is far less common[39]) want to devote their lives to taking care of their kids and their homes and decide to leave their careers behind, put them on pause, or to not pursue one from the start. Some spouses might support this idea, and some might want a working partner. Having a supportive partner is imperative to a spouse's success, whether at home or at work. There is no right or wrong answer, only what seems right to each couple. So it's important that partners agree on how they want to build a home and raise children (while also being clear on how many children they desire).

If you desire to pursue a career outside the home, research shows that your partner has a great influence over that success as well. A study done by Washington University with five thousand married people over the span of five years showed a positive correlation between having a supportive spouse and high workplace performance.[40] Having a spouse who's conscientious, along with other positive traits, attributed to the occupational success of the workers being evaluated. The study also showed that it is easier to maintain a productive work-life balance by having a spouse who helps keep your personal life running smoothly.

Couples where both partners have career aspirations have to be clear on how they will prioritize their ambitions, family time, and everything else that's important to them. In order to balance

---

39   Richard Fry, "Almost 1 in 5 Stay-at-Home Parents in the U.S. Are Dads," Pew Research Center, August 3, 2023, https://www.pewresearch.org/short-reads/2023/08/03/almost-1-in-5-stay-at-home-parents-in-the-us-are-dads/.

40   Gerry Everding, "Spouse's Personality Influences Career Success, Study Finds: Husbands, Wives May Influence Behavior in the Workplace," The Source, September 18, 2014, https://source.wustl.edu/2014/09/spouses-personality-influences-career-success-study-finds/.

everything, it's possible that one partner might have to sacrifice a dream or push it to the future in order to support the other in pursuing theirs, because their sacrifice will lead to success for the family unit. That success may come with many benefits, such as financial stability. But financial success isn't always a source of joy, it can also be a source of tension as you navigate how to manage it.

* * * * *

Can you guess the number one issue that married couples fight over? If you guessed finances, then you'd be right. Indeed, it is even the second leading cause of divorce after infidelity according to one study.[41]

Even before you start dating, you will have likely developed a particular relationship with money, and this will have a direct impact on your partnership because how you view and handle money influences how you make financial decisions. Having a scarcity mentality—thinking there is never enough money—will make you conscious of every dollar you spend. On the other hand, having an abundance mentality—thinking there is always enough money in the bank—will lead you to spend without calculating. These mentalities most likely developed from a young age based on how your family of origin viewed and managed money. For example, you might be thrifty if you grew up in a household where money was tight, but if you grew up around an overflow of money, you might have never needed to budget.

It's easy to manage your own money when no one else is involved, but managing money becomes a team effort when you get married—and that can create conflict when money mentalities clash. Engaged couples will get a small taste of this when they start

---

41   "Money Ruining Marriages in America: A Ramsey Solutions Study,"
      Ramsey Solutions, February 6, 2018, https://www.ramseysolutions.com
      /company/newsroom/releases/money-ruining-marriages-in-america.

wedding planning, as it will put their budgeting skills to the test and reveal how they treat money. So it's best to start thinking about how you each manage money as early as possible in the relationship. Dating couples can observe how their partner handles spending, saving, and debt. Also, sharing opinions about financial management can indicate how compatible you are with money.

While on the surface financial arguments might be about money, they aren't really just about money: They're about control and using your power. They're about secrecy and lack of transparency. They're about trusting your partner to make good financial decisions. And this is why money can create so much conflict in a relationship. When I got mad about spending more on our wedding invitations, it wasn't just about the money we'd have to pay. It was about being too proud to admit that I had made a mistake that, unfortunately, cost us a lot of money.

Also keep in mind that money can mean different things to men and women. How you feel about having "enough" money can be different from how your partner feels. According to research by Drs. John and Julie Gottman, women often equate "enough" money with love, respect, and security,[42] while men equate it to strength, independence, maturity, competition, social power, and winning. Further, you might have an expectation about how men and women should handle money in a relationship because of the way you saw your parents handle it growing up (assuming you come from a two-parent household) or from societal norms you observed. But money isn't the only thing you might have expectations around when it comes to gender roles.

---

42 John Gottman et al., *Eight Dates: Essential Conversations for a Lifetime of Love* (Hachette, UK: Workman Publishing Company, 2019), 128.

By nature, men and women have different qualities, strengths, and weaknesses. And in a relationship, their different communication styles, emotional needs, and behavioral tendencies can feel difficult to navigate. There are even books written about gender differences and how they can make you feel like men and women are from two completely different planets (the main message of the book *Men Are from Mars, Women Are from Venus*). So it is only natural that those differences will influence the role of each gender in a relationship.

Also, based on how you were raised, and from seeing the roles of fathers and mothers, you might have certain expectations about how you will share responsibilities and make decisions in your future home. Discussing topics such as the division of household tasks and chores will help you set realistic expectations for the future. Make sure to come to an agreement over the responsibility of raising children and how your lifestyle and careers will affect that. And have a plan for how you will work out your differences over significant decisions.

Cultural differences might also influence how you view gender roles. For example, coming from a patriarchal or matriarchal society will impact what you consider as normative roles for each gender. You should be able to identify some of these differences while dating and determine if you can work through them.

Being on the Same Page

Being on the same page with the five Fs of compatibility can be challenging, to say the least, but living in that space is highly rewarding, as are the ways you will grow both as individuals and as a couple as you navigate these differences. If they seem overwhelming, break them down even further and focus on the top ones that are most important to you, that you don't want to settle on. For example, you might be okay with not having the same leisure activities, but spiritual beliefs are nonnegotiable. Or you might be flexible on your relationship roles but have a strong stance on managing finances. Find out where you stand in each category with your partner before moving toward marriage. Ask all the questions you need to ask one another, and don't assume you know the answer based on your observations alone. And don't defer any hard conversations to after you're married because it might be too late then!

. . . . .

Here are some questions to help you evaluate your compatibility in a relationship:

- Do you and your partner share the same spiritual beliefs and observe the same religious practices?
- Are you and your partner comfortable sharing your feelings with one another, even when they are hard feelings that are difficult to open up about?
- When you share your feelings, do you feel heard and understood by your partner?
- Are you able to discuss problems in the relationship?
- Are you satisfied with the way you resolve conflicts?
- Do you enjoy spending time with your partner's friends and family?
- Do you have healthy boundaries to protect your relationship from potential interference from family and friends?
- Are you able to have fun with your partner and enjoy their company?
- Are there any personality traits your partner has that you have difficulty accepting?
- Are you concerned about how your partner manages money?

- Do you and your partner agree on how you will manage your money after marriage?
- Do you support each other's dreams and career aspirations?
- Do you agree on how many children you want and how you will raise them?
- Are you clear on how you will handle your responsibilities in your future household?
- Do you have a plan for how you will make decisions when you disagree with each other?

Myths about Compatibility

Myth #1: Our love can overcome any lack of compatibility.

Have you ever seen two people try their hardest to make their relationship work despite their apparent differences? They likely see ending their relationship as a sign of failure and want to desperately prove to everyone that they can make it work. They may ignore any wise advice you try to give them, and you cringe, watching them in their misery. Sometimes it's their pride that gets in the way of listening to their trusted guides, and other times it's the delusion that all they need is love.

"All You Need Is Love" is a catchy song, but relationships need more than just love—they need commitment and sacrifice—two things that are hard to do under typical circumstances and even harder to practice in a relationship that lacks compatibility. In these situations, all your effort and energy will go toward constantly working out your differences. You will spend most of your time trying to survive and have very little energy left to thrive as a couple. It takes humility to admit things aren't working out and bravery to break up. I pray you find those two things if and when the time calls for it.

Myth #2: It's impossible to find good compatibility, so I have to settle.

Finding 100 percent compatibility is impossible, but finding compatibility that's good enough to make a relationship work is possible. Compatibility can still be found among differences, and these differences can complement one another and fill in the gaps you have as individuals. This will be the case if your core values, beliefs, and goals align. But if any of the significant things you need in a relationship aren't present (recall the list you made in chapter 3), don't settle. If you are constantly in conflict and can't communicate well, don't settle. If the way you live out your faith is different from the way your partner does it, don't settle. If the things you honor and cherish are not meaningful to your partner, don't settle.

And the one major thing you should never settle on is marrying someone who cannot lead you to the Kingdom. If marriage is your path to salvation, then you want a partner to help you and your family on the journey. You can compromise on the less weighty things that won't matter in the long run, and if you don't know yet how to distinguish those things from the important things, ask the married people in your circle of guidance. Your partner's good looks and charm will fade over time, and individual tastes, hobbies, and preferences may change, but their relationship with God should grow.

Myth #3: I won't be able to find a better partner than this one.

I do encourage this way of thinking when you're in the right relationship and are ready to settle down. When you're dating someone who's checking off the right boxes, it's good to look no further and commit to the relationship. But if you find yourself saying this with hesitation, knowing in your gut that something is wrong, then I want you to reconsider the relationship and steer clear of this myth.

You might know deep down that this isn't the right person for you because of your lack of compatibility and frequent conflicts. But instead of walking away, you want to white-knuckle through the conflict, afraid your current relationship is as good as it gets. This comes from having a scarcity mentality around dating. You might believe that there aren't many good people out there for you to date. Well, I have news for you, if you keep telling yourself that, then it becomes a self-fulfilling prophesy. Whenever you meet someone new you will have already jumped to the conclusion that they're not good enough, and never give them a chance. You get in your own way of happiness by doing this. But if you believe there are good people out there, you will be able to see them when you meet them. Don't stay with a partner who is lacking many things because of fear that you won't find anyone better.

6

Make It or Break It

If you date to figure out if someone would be a suitable partner and eventually a spouse for you, sometimes the answer is yes, and sometimes the answer is no. When the answer is no, then the next right step is to break up. If you've ever experienced a breakup, you know how devastating it can feel, especially after a long-term relationship. It can feel like your world, full of hopes and dreams, is crashing down. The future you envisioned disappears instantly, and you cannot grasp what is happening. You have to say goodbye to months or years of shared memories. And coping with the unknown future, void of the person you envisioned it with, can be overwhelming. That, my friends, is the unfortunate part of dating.

Sometimes you might be able to see a breakup coming because you sense things are going downhill. And other times you might feel blindsided because you thought things were going well. If a breakup takes you by surprise, it could be because the other person did not do a great job of sharing how they were feeling, or because you've been wearing rose-colored glasses, seeing things as if they were better than they were in reality.

Take Off the Rose-Colored Glasses

You might find yourself bringing out your best pair of rose-colored glasses when you're trying hard to make a relationship work. These glasses make you perceive situations as much better than they actually are, and you might use them because you are tired of being single and you would rather ignore warning signs and stay in a relationship than be lonely. Or you might feel like you're running out of time to find a spouse, and so you turn a blind eye to all the relationship's flaws for the sake of getting married.

Early in a relationship, there's also a risk that you will be blinded by infatuation, which can lead you to miss a lot of vital warning signs. The bright, blinking warning lights can become dim and faint, or you can mistake them for dazzling lights. You can also get caught up daydreaming about the future and miss what's right in front of you: you'll find yourself already planning your Pinterest-worthy wedding day and failing to plan for the marriage.

Usually, once the dating honeymoon phase is over, your infatuation will fade and the reality of the relationship, specifically an unhealthy one, will catch you like a deer in headlights bracing for impact. All the bandages of sweet words you placed on hurtful interactions will fall off and leave wounds at risk of being infected if not treated properly. At that point you may either become disillusioned with the relationship, or you may try to keep the rose-colored glasses on even tighter to keep you from seeing the negative reality. But it's important to see things as they really are, and to decide whether the relationship is worth working on or whether it's time to say goodbye.

To figure out whether you should buckle down and do the work, or head for the hills, don't date in a bubble and cut yourself off from the outside world. Let others into the relationship—mainly your circle of guidance. The people you trust the most won't be blinded by love the way you might be: an outside perspective can offer you the correct perception you might be missing. Someone else can help you spot red flags and toxic traits that are undetectable because of your rose-colored glasses.

Identifying Red Flags and Toxic Relationships

Even before you start dating, as you list what you're looking for in a partner also list things you would consider red flags. But keep in mind that some red flags won't surface until you've gotten to know the person more while dating, so it's important to keep an eye out for these things as you go along, and compare it against your list of red flags. It's helpful to refer back to your written list as your relationship progresses, as it will allow you to clearly assess the situation.

As everyone's list of dating criteria will look different, so will the red flag list because you might be able to tolerate certain things that others cannot and vice versa. But there are some things that no one should have to live with, such as dishonesty, disrespect, substance abuse, uncontrolled temper, and any form of abuse—verbal, physical, or emotional.[43]

And generally, if you're looking for someone with qualities that resemble the fruit of the Spirit, then the red flags you want to avoid are the opposite characteristics. Here is a detailed list St. Paul mentions right before He writes about the fruit of the Spirit:

Now the works of the flesh are evident, which are: adultery, fornication, uncleanness, lewdness, idolatry, sorcery, hatred, contentions, jealousies, outbursts of wrath, selfish ambitions,

---

43   Fileta, *True Love Dates: Your Indispensable Guide to Finding the Love of Your Life*, 63.

dissensions, heresies, envy, murders, drunkenness, revelries, and the like; of which I tell you beforehand, just as I also told *you* in time past, that those who practice such things will not inherit the kingdom of God. (Gal. 5:19–21)

A partner exhibiting these behaviors will hinder you from your ultimate goal in marriage: inheriting the Kingdom. These traits might sound a little extreme, and you might be thinking, *of course, I won't date a sorcerer or murderer,* but they might have toxic traits that are more subtle than these. We all have flaws, but if we leave them unattended, those flaws can morph into toxic behaviors and habits. If you find yourself dating someone who makes you feel worse about yourself and whose behavior adds negativity to the relationship, it might be a sign that you're in a toxic relationship. The most obvious sign is if you experience any form of abuse and you don't feel safe. Abuse is an extreme form of toxicity, and if this is your experience, please talk to a trusted professional and get help immediately.

Here are more signs to help you determine if you are in a toxic relationship:

- You feel like your partner is manipulative and controlling.
- You're afraid to express your concerns because your partner will place the blame on you.
- You feel judged and belittled in the relationship.
- Your partner rarely takes ownership of issues you point out and doesn't address them.
- When you feel hurt, your partner dismisses your feelings and shows no empathy.
- You feel your partner is trying to isolate you from your friends and family.

- Your partner needs your attention constantly and becomes enraged when they cannot reach you.
- Your partner disappears for long periods of time without explanation.

As no relationship is perfect, you might experience these behaviors occasionally, or your relationship might go through short seasons that are bumpy. But what determines if your relationship is unhealthy for short periods or is generally toxic is the severity and frequency of these behaviors. If you're dating someone who demonstrates these behaviors often and either has no interest in changing, or keeps promising to change but shows no improvement, you might be dating a toxic person. If they slip up occasionally and take ownership of their faults and intentionally change, it might result from their personal flaws rather than from a toxic trait. On the other hand, you might be the one demonstrating these behaviors, making you the toxic one in the relationship. Pay attention to what your partner reveals to you, and note anything you need to work on.

Remember, too, that actions speak louder than words. Your partner's ill-treatment of you is a sign of deep-rooted issues they need to work on, and working through them might require a break from the relationship. You don't have to be a martyr and put up with unacceptable behavior, hoping that your presence in the relationship will save them. Only they have the power to change themselves, by God's grace.

A friend once described to me what it felt like to be in a toxic relationship: "I would wake up anxious and scared. I felt like I was holding my breath the entire time, not knowing what hurtful thing he might say or do next. He was controlling, and nothing I ever did pleased him." She admitted, "I felt such a relief when we broke up, and I don't know why I stayed in that relationship for so long." But that's the grip a toxic relationship can have, making you feel like you can't get out, so you stay and hope things will miraculously get better. If a relationship is the reason you are fighting anxiety, or experiencing panic attacks, then the cure is to end that relationship. You're not married yet and have not committed to staying together for better or for worse. You are not beholden to your significant other. If after you have diligently tried to improve things and there is no change, then the choice to walk away is within your power (and much easier to do before marriage).

To Stay or to Go?

When evaluating a relationship, you want to see it for what it is in the present, not for what you hope it can be. You'll need to take into account what you've learned in this book, from characteristics you want in a mate and if you're compatible, to whether the person displays any red flags or toxic traits. Don't date someone for their potential, hoping you might change them; rather, be with them for who they currently are. Individually and as a couple, you should certainly aim for growth and self-improvement, but that is not always guaranteed.

A compatible and healthy foundation will help you evolve and grow in the same direction. As the years roll by, growing responsibilities will press in at different stages of life, making change inevitable, and priorities might shift to accommodate newfound circumstances. If you start with little compatibility, signs of toxicity, or multiple red flags, your relationship's chance for flourishing, and for withstanding change, isn't promising.

Additionally, when you're trying to decide whether to stay or go, keep in mind that someone might sound like an excellent fit for you on paper, but as you start dating, you might realize you lack compatibility. While you may have things in common, the differences in your personalities might be why you're unable to get along easily. Relationships, without a doubt, require work, but everything shouldn't feel like an uphill battle. Dating should be enjoyable and even simple. When a relationship is compatible, happiness will come naturally as you put in the typical work required, but you won't have to work overtime to achieve the peace you want in a relationship. What if the relationship isn't working, despite the amount of work you're putting into it? It may be a sign that it's time to let go.

Dealing with Breakups

When I first started providing relationship coaching for young adults, I thought I'd be helping them navigate dating or making things work with the right partner, but what I didn't envision was how many clients I would coach through or after a breakup. I remember when Julia came to me, a successful and beautiful woman, heartbroken that her boyfriend of nearly two years had broken up with her. They were a great match on paper, coming from similar backgrounds and having the same interests and goals. She thought they were heading toward marriage, but he saw things differently. As she took the time to grieve the end of the relationship, we spent time in our sessions observing why things didn't go according to plan.

As painful as some of the conversations were, through her tears and reflections, she realized there were many things in the relationship that were not okay, and because of her commitment to wanting to make things work, she had brushed them off. The flaws she dismissed were clear signs of their lack of compatibility and, ultimately, what drove them apart. We discussed what she had learned from her experience and what she would look out for in the next relationship. It wasn't an overnight process, but Julia ultimately made peace with the fact that he was not the right person for her, and she was able to move forward.

Like Julia did, when you say goodbye to a partner, take the time you need to grieve the end of the relationship. Don't dodge those painful feelings and jump right into another relationship so you can distract yourself from feeling the heartache. Doing this will only mean you are in a relationship "on the rebound," and that usually doesn't work out well. And remember, you're not only grieving the person you lost, but also the future you imagined and the foundation you built together, and that takes time. You'll have to face the discomfort, but you don't need to let it overtake you and leave you in despair. By the grace of God, you will be able to move on.

If you feel like you've hit a dead end and cannot find the light at the end of the tunnel, therapy or coaching can help you gain clarity. Also, leaning on your circle of guidance during this time can be extremely helpful. They would have been there since the relationship's inception and thus can help you define what led to the breakup. They can also help you recognize and break any unhealthy cycles that might exist. Don't be too quick to blame the other person for any unhealthy cycles and problems; there is always room for self-improvement (or at least improvement in choosing who you date and how you date). It's important to spend time reflecting on the relationship and what role you played in it, so that you can learn from your mistakes and do better next time.

Even when they don't last, relationships will always help you learn something, and this is part of why I don't believe there are failed relationships, only relationships that end and relationships that continue. And since relationships are meant to guide you to your spouse, if they bring you to the right person, they succeed. But if they take you away from the wrong person, they also succeed. Marriage is a covenant not meant to be broken, so it's better when relationships end before this point—though unfortunately, we live in a broken world, and divorce is a reality for some. Therefore, I want you to put the most effort into your premarital relationships to prepare for an unbreakable marriage (but even if you find yourself in a broken marriage, remember God's grace is there for you too, whether you choose to stay or to go).

While you can't avoid breakups, there is a way you can make them less painful—by leaving the sexual component out of dating, so that you're simply getting to know someone. As you will read in the next chapter, being sexually active complicates things and makes it harder to walk away from a relationship that isn't right for you. Dating is about collecting the facts you need to make a logical decision on whether to move forward or not. As you see the relationship going in the right direction, trust will slowly begin to grow and the emotional components will come. Don't get attached to someone too quickly before evaluating the facts and getting to know who they really are.

It also helps to set some guidelines as you start to date, in case you break up, so that you're on the same page if things don't work out. Decide if you'd prefer to stay friends, acquaintances, or go your separate ways. Have a plan for how you will handle things if you run into each other again. Planning for this might sound counterproductive, but it will help you navigate uncomfortable future situations, especially if your lives are intertwined on some level (e.g., you have mutual friends, attend the same parish, or work for the same company).

You can also be intentional about making decisions in specific time frames. In my opinion, after about three to six months of dating you should know someone's personality well enough to see if you want to continue seriously pursuing them. You might know sooner if it's easy to spot incompatibility or red flags right from the start. Often, after around a year of dating you can better know if marriage is where you're heading. Don't rush into making that marriage decision after a few short months of dating and before you get to know your partner fully. These general guidelines can be shorter or longer based on different factors, such as how frequently you see each other, long-distance dating, and direction from your circle of guidance. This can be something you internally set for yourself or agree on as a couple.

While this isn't an exact science, some find that setting guidelines relieves some pressure. Instead of jumping to conclusions after every date, you get to enjoy the getting-to-know-each-other period. The process becomes less about decision-making at every step and more about giving each other a solid chance before evaluating the entire relationship.

If a relationship doesn't end up working out and you have to experience the pain of a breakup, trust in God and His healing grace and mercy, and trust that "all things work together for good to those who love God, to those who are the called according to *His* purpose" (Rom. 8:28). We don't just hope or wish that setbacks will work for good, we *know* they will.

Myths about Breakups

Myth #1: We can't break up because we've invested so much in the relationship.

Investing in a relationship takes a lot from you: your time, effort, emotions, money, and more—so after months or even years of being with someone, it might be hard to imagine your life without them. And how intertwined your lives have become makes it hard to go your separate ways, especially if you've been physically intimate. You might be afraid of jumping off into the unknown, and that fear is keeping you from letting go. But staying in the wrong relationship is likely worse than anything coming in the future. It's difficult to leave a relationship but even harder to stay in the wrong one. Choose the level of difficulty you want to deal with.

Instead of only seeing a breakup as a negative thing, consider the positive things that can come out of it. Examining what went wrong will help you learn what to avoid in the future. If the relationship reveals things you need to change then you can challenge yourself to change for the better. It also means that you're one step closer to finding the right person by eliminating one that wasn't right for you.

Myth #2: If I stay in this relationship long enough, things will get better.

Although this sounds like a hopeful statement, oftentimes it is a false one. It's good to strive for improvement in a relationship. But if you've tried and tried countless times and things are still not getting better, the chances of improvement are slim to none. Be honest with yourself about the state of your relationship and assess it for where it currently is, not where you hope it will go.

Gabriella experienced this myth the hard way. She was in a shaky relationship that had its good moments but really low moments too. She was growing tired of the dating scene and desperately wanted to settle down and start a family. Her boyfriend looked great on paper: he had a lot going for him and possessed many of the things she was looking for in a partner, except something was off with the way he made her feel. He made her feel inadequate: nothing she did was good enough for him or the relationship. They would constantly argue but try to forgive each other and move past the fight without implementing any real solutions.

Gabriella's friends and the major players of her circle of guidance expressed serious concern over her relationship. But she loved her boyfriend, and she claimed they didn't know him like she did. She also felt like she was running out of time as she was getting older and had already invested so much in the relationship. Despite the disapproval of her circle of guidance, she headed toward marriage with him, telling herself that time would make things better, especially after this new level of commitment. But we know that marriage doesn't solve problems, it typically magnifies them. And that is exactly what happened.

They got married and the arguments got louder, the bad feelings got worse, and the fights kept on coming. Gabriella has sought professional help to improve her marriage; it's an uphill battle she continues to fight. But God's grace has carried her through it thus far and will continue to.

Myth #3: No one will want me after I end a long-term relationship.

If we understand that breaking up might be a natural outcome of dating, then there shouldn't be such a stigma around it. When clients tell me that this is a fear they have, I push back and tell them not to make decisions for other people. When you start to believe this myth, you're judging yourself and others as well. You assume that you're not good enough for anyone else and put yourself down. And you're jumping to conclusions by assuming others won't be open-minded and understanding about your past situations. Please don't think in this way. It leaves no room for God's grace and His ability to redeem your past.

Don't fear a breakup because you think it will be hard, or even impossible, to enter another relationship. Don't worry about what others will say or how your reputation will be perceived. You worship a God who has turned sinners into evangelists, transformed harlots into saints, and made murderers into leaders; surely nothing is too great for Him to change.

PART 3

The Struggle

A Note from the Author

Before you read the third part of the book, I want you to know that my goal is not to overwhelm you with rules and guidelines or to make you feel any sort of shame or guilt. I simply want to highlight the instructions God has given us through His holy Word and shed light on how we ought to live. Neither I nor God expect you to live a perfect life, but a life that consists of rising back up after you fall down.

If you feel like purity and holiness are a far reach for you because of your past, then I recommend starting with chapter 10 first. I want to encourage you to rise up and keep reaching for the standard God has set for you, because the struggle is worth it!

7

Pursuing Purity

"I just have so many regrets from this past relationship," a client once told me in tears during a coaching session. She proceeded to explain how she had allowed herself to cross some physical boundaries she initially had set with her ex, and she was feeling immense regret over it. Another client told me he was afraid to enter a new relationship, worried that the mistakes of his past would follow him like a lurking shadow. He feared a future potential partner would reject him because of his lack of "purity." I assured these clients that the repentance and confession they had gone through had surely erased their mistakes, but their struggle against regret was still evident.

These clients echoed the same feelings of shame, guilt, and regret I have heard from so many other men and women. They, as well as I, were taught and grew up believing that a person's value is found in their purity, which is directly tied to acts of physical intimacy they engage in before they are married. While I was growing up in the Church I heard many analogies for purity, and quite a few were shame-filled. Here are just a few (paraphrased) examples:

131

- "You are like a sticky piece of tape. When you stick to dirt by taking part in inappropriate relationships, you lose your stickiness. And when it's time for marriage, you won't be able to stick to the right person—your future spouse."
- "You are like a treasure chest full of beautiful treasures. Whenever you give a piece of your heart or purity to a guy, you're giving another of your treasures away. Then, when you meet your future husband, you won't have any treasures remaining, and you will have very little left to offer him."
- "You are like a new, fresh piece of paper. If you crumple up the paper and try to flatten it out again, it will never return to its initial clean, crisp state. It's the same with your purity: Once you lose it, you will never be able to get it back."

There are plenty more analogies, but I think you get the point. I know many women reading this, no matter what their religious upbringing, will nod their heads, testifying to similar experiences—while men might be hearing it for the first time. Or worse, men might have heard it before and grown to believe that if a woman compromises her purity she is "damaged goods" (a term I cringe at hearing) and should be dismissed as a potential wife. Another problem is that since many Christian men were probably spared these incorrect teachings (at least, that's what most of the men I know have admitted to), this has caused an unfair double standard to exist. Purity was emphasized as a virtue a woman must possess if she desired marriage, yet a man might be able to get away with an impure past without any consequences.

I do not doubt that the youth leaders repeating these examples were well-intentioned and simply looking out for us. And if I'm being honest, I also used them in my early years of ministry, until I began to understand the potential harm of doing so. Warnings like these may even work fine for some people who are obedient rule-followers and never compromise their purity. But the fact is, these warnings are rooted in fear and shame, and they leave people who have made mistakes feeling shame and believing they are beyond repair.

I hope by now you are beginning to recognize the danger of oversimplifying purity to analogies like those listed above. They limit purity to a series of actions you must take or refrain from, completely ignoring the depth and complexity of living a sanctified life. They reduce impurity merely to losing one's virginity or engaging in other premarital sexual acts. They also leave little room for repentance, confession, grace, and for God to make all things new through His love and mercy. Instead, they drill into our minds that our sinful actions lead to destruction and that there is no room for a redemptive U-turn (more on this in chapter 10).

Not only are these warnings too extreme, but according to them, the moral of the story is always that you should guard your purity for your future spouse. And if you "give your purity away" to someone, nothing will be left for your spouse, and you most likely will be unwanted. But purity is not specifically for a future spouse; it is so you can honor God and carry yourself as the temple He dwells in. Purity is for now and forever, single or married, young or old. And while there's no question that purity plays a fundamental role in romantic relationships, ideally, this foundation is laid years before one begins dating. When we are single, pursuing purity should be an ongoing journey that has deep roots in self-control and godliness. And this journey doesn't end once we find our spouse: purity and chastity ought to be cornerstones of every marriage.

Additionally, from an Orthodox lens, it's inaccurate to think that you can "give your purity away." Purity is an ongoing effort that requires cooperation between ourselves and God, leading to sanctification. Sin threatens our sanctification and aims to separate us from God, so compromising purity is a tragedy, not because we cross a physical boundary with someone who is not our spouse, nor even because we lose our virginity, but because it robs us of communion with Christ. Even if we wait until marriage, we don't "give our purity away" to our spouse; that would imply we become impure by partaking of sexual acts in marriage, which is entirely incorrect.

What does it even mean to be "pure," then? While the Merriam-Webster Dictionary offers several definitions, the one that most resonates with the focus of this chapter describes it as "containing nothing that does not properly belong."[44] This phrase offers a framework for understanding the complex concept of purity. To truly understand the concept, we need to return to the beginning: when God first formed human beings in the garden, they were a pure creation, not yet infiltrated by sin. His initial design for humanity was perfect, yet we altered our sanctified state by our actions. Pride, envy, jealously, murder, lust, and other sins began tainting our initial pure state. These things did not properly belong in God's initial creation of us, and as a consequence they led to separation from Him. We went from a life of glorious harmony with God and creation in the Garden of Eden to one of toil and suffering. In a fallen world, regaining sanctification became a struggle that would take us a lifetime to achieve and was only made possible by the redemption gained through Christ's Incarnation, death, and Resurrection.

Returning to our pure state is no easy task. Removing the toxins that have made their way into our life can be difficult. Yet it is the only way back to holiness and a struggle we must face, especially in relationships, as we work to flee sexual immorality (and also as we

---

44 *Merriam-Webster*, s.v. "pure (a.)," accessed April 8, 2023,
    https://www.merriam-webster.com/dictionary/pure.

strive to avoid other sins that get in the way of treating our partner with love, grace, respect, etc.).

Being Aware of Our Flaws

As we struggle to live a pure life, we have to first make sure we are aware of our own flaws so that we know what we must struggle against. Imagine trying to get ready in the early dark hours of the morning, but you don't want to wake anyone else in your house, so you don't turn on any lights and get dressed in the dark. I often do this when I wake up early for work and don't want to disturb my husband or kids. Sometimes I resort to my lightly worn pile of clothes that I've placed in some corner of my room. Those clothes aren't straight out of the wash but are not dirty enough to be put in the laundry bin. As I make my way out the door, into my car, and to my office, somewhere along the way, I realize I have a stain on my shirt or a patch of dirt on my pants. I couldn't see it earlier because I chose to get dressed in the dark, and the blemishes only became apparent when exposed to the light.

It's the same way with our souls. When we are away from the true light, we miss many flaws, and they go undetected for too long until they wreak havoc on our lives. We can only identify those imperfections in the presence of illumination, and the Bible is essential for this. God's instructions are the light we need to see our weaknesses. The more time we spend trying to know God through His Word and striving to live according to His commands, the closer we get to the light that exposes the darkness. Living in the darkness won't do us any good, especially as we struggle on the path to eternity, and ignoring the commands that seem difficult to live out might seem easier in the short run, but that trajectory will place us in destructive darkness.

If we choose to ignore our flaws and refuse to work on them, this will lead us into sin, and the ultimate consequence of sin is death and a life away from God. So God calls us to flee sexual immortality (1 Cor. 6:18) not because He's cruel and doesn't want us to have any fun, but because He loves us and wants to protect us from the negative consequences, as any loving father would. We know that He loves us greatly, because He even went as far as to be crucified to set us free from the bondage of sin. He longs for us to return to our pure and unaltered state so that we can join Him in Paradise, which is why His instructions and biblical commands construct a carefully thought-out plan to return us to our union with Him. And His commandments are not meant to be burdensome; it's the opposite. They are liberating because they free us from being held captive by sin: "For this is the love of God, that we keep His commandments. And His commandments are not burdensome. For whatever is born of God overcomes the world. And this is the victory that has overcome the world—our faith" (1 John 5:3–4).

When I became a parent, I began to better understand why following God's commands were crucial to my spiritual survival and growth. When my kids were little, I showered them with love and affection, but I also had rules for them: they couldn't touch the stove, play with knives, go near electric outlets, etc. Was I a cruel parent who wanted to limit their curiosity and fun? No, I wanted to protect them from getting burned, cut, electrocuted, or worse. No adult would argue with these rules or deem them unreasonable. And God is even more loving and protective than any human parent; that is the kind of Father He is. He sees what will hurt us and warns us to stay away because what might seem innocent and fun in the moment can have long-term harmful effects.

If I let my toddler cut vegetables with a sharp knife, although it may be exciting for her to cut them so neatly and powerfully, chances are her little fingers will get cut, and maybe even permanently scarred. Someday she will be able to use the knife safely but not until she is older and more mature. Similarly, there is a proper time and place for many of us to express our sexual desires (within the context of marriage), and it will be beautiful and holy. But acting on this too soon—when we are single or dating—will leave wounds that need much care to cure.

Fleeing Sexual Immorality

The Scripture is full of instructions on how to live purely and avoid sin, and one major way we can remain pure according to the Bible and the Christian faith is by abstaining from sexual immorality. The next question then becomes, what is sexual immorality? Is it fornication: sex outside of marriage? Is it adultery: sexual relations with someone besides your spouse? Is it other premarital sexual acts? What if I told you the answer is all of the above, and more? The standard Christ sets is so much deeper than these measures; the above indicators are mainly just symptoms of underlying immorality. Christ indicates this in Matthew 5:27–28 when He tells us, "You have heard that it was said to those of old, 'You shall not commit adultery.' But I say to you that whoever looks at a woman to lust for her has already committed adultery with her in his heart." Here, He challenges us to see purity not just as avoiding a sinful action but as an intention of the heart and mind. Impure actions do not just happen out of the blue; they stem from being planted and watered in our hearts and minds. Our thoughts encompass our desires until they motivate our actions.

So purity is not simply a box you check off if you haven't had premarital sex. Indeed, even many saints were not virgins, yet they reached a state of spiritual purity higher than most (e.g., St. Mary of Egypt). It isn't about drawing a line around what you're willing to do or not do physically. It's about intention as much as it is about action. It's about living a chaste life, and chastity is an attitude you live by pursuing purity in both conduct *and* intention. And purity and chastity are a way of life beyond marriage, not just something to pursue in the interim.

Even though purity is not completely about virginity, virginity does help us remain pure, and it prevents us from binding ourselves to the wrong person. St. Paul explains the consequences of having sex with the wrong person, knowing that the physical act of sex has a bonding and uniting effect: "Do you not know that your bodies are members of Christ? Shall I then take the members of Christ and make *them* members of a harlot? Certainly not! Or do you not know that he who is joined to a harlot is one body *with her*? For 'the two,' He says, 'shall become one flesh'" (1 Cor. 6:15–16). Sex is powerful, as God intended it to be, and if handled without care and caution, it can lead to our downfall, which will take hard work to rise up from. Be wise and cautious with this beautiful gift that God has given us.

Even if you are being cautious, you might find that it's still very difficult to flee from sexual immorality in the pursuit of purity and chastity because the world may laugh at your intentions to remain pure. David the Psalmist attests to this by saying, "The proud have me in great derision, / *Yet* I do not turn aside from Your law" (Ps. 119:51). Satan will try to leverage that mockery to convince you to give into temptation, so you must have immovable convictions of what God has called you to and stand firm without lowering your standards.

Sure, modern society may regard purity as an outdated or old-fashioned value, sometimes under the guise that sex is necessary to build a strong relationship. But these are lies that drown out a more profound truth: We are not of the world (John 15:19); there-fore, we must not act according to the world's standards. And we are not looking for the rewards of this world but the coming eternal world God has prepared for us. Aristides, a first-century Athenian Christian philosopher, observed: "Christian women are chaste, kind and gentle. The men refrain from all unlawful intimate relationships. They keep free of all impurity, for they live in expectation of the rewards of the other world."[45] It should be the same for us who follow Christ two millennia later.

It's also important to remember that we are sinning not only against God when we commit sexual immorality but against our own flesh and soul. Saint Paul tells us this when he says: "Flee sexual immorality. Every sin that a man does is outside the body, but he who commits sexual immorality sins against his own body" (1 Cor. 6:18). Commenting on this verse, one Church Father wrote, "Fornication is a sin of the body which touches both the body and the soul."[46] So while sin damages our souls, and some sin may hurt our bodies, giving in to sexual immorality will harm both.

We also have to keep in mind that our bodies are not ours alone, as St. Paul continues to write in 1 Corinthians 6, "Or do you not know that your body is the temple of the Holy Spirit *who is* in you, whom you have from God, and you are not your own? For you were bought at a price; therefore glorify God in your body and in your spirit, which are God's" (vv. 19–20). Once we understand that our bodies are not our own and were bought at a price, we realize that we are merely the caretakers of something valuable lent to us. Contrary to what modern society believes, our bodies belong to Him, the One who created them. God has entrusted us to care for them and keep them pure. If we do not care for our bodies in a holy and righteous

---

45   Fr. George W. Grube, *What the Church Fathers Say About . . .* 2 vols. (Minneapolis, MN: Light & Life Publishing Company, 2005), 66.

46   Gerald Bray, *1-2 Corinthians: Ancient Christian Commentary*, NT, vol. 7 (Downers Grove, IL: InterVarsity Press, 1999), 56.

way, we will experience the consequences that follow. This is the law of sin, and we know that sin brings forth death (James 1:15).

Consequences of Sexual Immorality

So we see that when we commit sexual immorality, we sin with our whole being—body, mind, and spirit. Therefore, the toll sexual sin takes on us comes in many different forms—spiritual, physical, and emotional. The most critical of these is the spiritual because with this, we separate ourselves from God, the only One who can truly heal and restore us.

We might not intentionally set out to separate ourselves from God, but that is the spiritual consequence of sexual immorality, as it is with any sin. One missed step after another can lead us down a path far away from Him; it becomes a slow fade without us even noticing. The devil loves it when we slowly drift away, so he tempts us with a tiny sin that may not seem like a big deal, but then we move on to the next one, and they get bigger each time. His lies and deception lead to our spiritual captivity, and this is why St. Paul tells us not to give the devil an opportunity (Eph. 4:27 [ESV]). Once the enemy has the smallest foothold on our soul, he'll kick the door wide open, enticing us into greater deceptions.

Sexual immorality can also have serious physical consequences, such as STIs or STDs (sexually transmitted infections or diseases), including HIV or AIDS,[47] and/or unplanned pregnancies. In 2022, there were more than 2.5 million cases of syphilis, gonorrhea, and chlamydia reported in the United States,[48] and having multiple sex-

---

47 "STDs and HIV – CDC Basic Fact Sheet," CDC, April 12, 2022, https://www.cdc.gov/sti/?CDC_AAref_Val=https://www.cdc.gov/std/hiv/stdfact-std-hiv.htm.

48 "Sexually Transmitted Infections Surveillance, 2022," CDC, January 30, 2024, https://www.cdc.gov/std/statistics/2022/default.htm.

ual partners increases the rate of contracting these infections. Even if you are only sleeping with one person, they might not be doing the same (or they may have had multiple past partners), and therefore your risk can be high. These STIs can cause serious, long-term medical issues if not treated, and they are sure to cause short-term pain and discomfort.

In 2019, the unintended pregnancy rate in the US was 35.7 pregnancies per one thousand women ages 15–44.[49] And in 2020, the teen birth rate was 15.4 births for every one thousand females ages 15–19.[50] We must realize that pregnancy is a possible, natural result of sex, and that there is a chance of it happening, despite using common birth control methods (because not all are 100 percent effective). Therefore, we must be ready to embrace that outcome every time we engage in sexual intercourse.

While pregnancy and STDs are possible physical consequences of sex, there is another that is more subtle than those: the chemical attachment to a partner. Oxytocin, a hormone known as the "love hormone," is produced by the hypothalamus and released during acts of human bonding such as sexual intercourse, hugging, cuddling, and a mother breastfeeding her child. Sex can stimulate oxytocin release in both men and women.[51] God intended sex to be a way for husbands and wives to bond to one another, forming a strong attachment, but when it happens outside of marriage, sex still has

49 "U.S. Pregnancy Rates Drop During Last Decade," CDC, April 12, 2023, https://www.cdc.gov/nchs/pressroom/nchs_press_releases/2023/20230412 .htm#:~:text=Unintended%20pregnancy%20rates%20declined%20by ,ending%20in%20abortion%20declined%2017%25.

50 Michelle J.K. Osterman et al., "Births: Final Data for 2020," *National Vital Statistics Reports* 70, no. 17, https://www.cdc.gov/nchs/data/nvsr/nvsr70/ nvsr70-17.pdf.

51 Bruce White and Susan Porterfield, *Endocrine and Reproductive Physiology* (Philadelphia, PA: Elsevier, 2013), 108.

that bonding effect. So if you become physically intimate with the wrong person, it becomes that much harder to detach when you need to. This brings us into another realm of consequences: emotional.

Emotional attachment might not be something you can tangibly measure, but it is something you can deeply feel. The more you open yourself up to someone, the more emotionally attached you become, and physical intimacy takes that attachment to a whole new level. That attachment is meant for a spouse that you are tied to for life, so if you realize the person you're sleeping with isn't the right person for you, the breakup is going to be felt deeper. Breaking up with someone is hard, but breaking up with someone you've had sex with is even harder. So having sex outside of marriage, where there is no mutual commitment to one another before God, leaves you more vulnerable to heartbreak. Some who want to avoid this heartbreak try to detach sex from emotions, which in turn devalues the sacredness of sex and creates more problems than solutions, as it can lead to issues later in marriage where sex won't hold the high value it should because of how it was treated in the past.

But do not be discouraged if you have fallen into temptation and experienced any of these consequences. Sin is inevitable due to our fallen state, as it is written in Romans, "for all have sinned and fall short of the glory of God" (3:23). At one point or another we have all fallen short of the glory of God, whether because of sexual sins or other sins.

The Challenges of Staying Pure

At this point, you may be thinking that being pure isn't exactly a satisfying way to live, and you are right that pursuing chastity and resisting your sexual urges is hardly a trivial task. It may even feel at times, as St. Mark the Ascetic puts it, that "living a chaste

Christian life is sometimes more difficult than suffering a martyr's death."[52] And there's no way around it: sex is pleasurable—that's how God intended it to be. And I can't lie and say that premarital physical intimacy is *always* terrible. It's enticing to want to connect to another person in that way, and to want to feel the physical high and experience the rush of dopamine (the pleasure chemical). But don't be fooled; as we have seen in this chapter, that instant physical pleasure will leave burn marks in its tracks. In fact, it's better not even to taste it in the first place. Because once you do, you might be tempted to come back to it again and again. It's harder to crave something you've never tasted.

It's also difficult to stay pure because the truth is, sex does feel good at the time: instant gratification is undeniably enjoyable. And living in a world where everything can be available to us instantly wires us to expect quick results. We often rush from one thing to another, satisfying our every desire. We're always chasing after the next big thing, and once we get it, our amusement with it is short-lived and we find ourselves chasing something new.

Due to the challenges of living in this kind of world, I have heard many young people complain that no one is pure anymore, and they're not entirely wrong. The CDC reported in 2017 that an estimated 55 percent of male and female teens had sexual intercourse by age eighteen.[53] Another survey administered by the CDC in 2019 showed that fewer than 40 percent of American high schoolers had sexual intercourse, a decline of over fifteen percentage points

---

52 Grube, *What the Church Fathers Say About . . .* , 66.
53 "Over Half of U.S. Teens Have Had Sexual Intercourse by Age 18, New Report Shows," CDC, June 22, 2017, https://www.cdc.gov/nchs /pressroom/nchs_press_releases/2017/201706_NSFG.htm#:~:text=An%20 estimated%2055%25%20of%20male,for%20Health%20Statistics%20 (NCHS).

since the early 1990s.[54] Statistics collected from 2011 to 2015 by the National Survey of Family Growth showed that 89 percent of women (15–44 years of age) and 90 percent of men (20–44 years of age) have had premarital sex.[55] Those are alarmingly high percentages, and if you don't have your eyes set on Christ, it is easy to give in to these societal norms. Our faith does not teach self-indulgence and instant gratification; rather, it points to the need for self-control, long-suffering, and patience. Instant rewards are promises made by the world, which isn't concerned with our long-term spiritual life or salvation.

Beyond instant gratification and physical pleasure, remaining pure is particularly challenging once you are in a committed relationship and long to express love for your partner in a physical way. It's normal to want to match words of affection with affectionate touches, especially with a partner that you're attracted to, and having an innate sex drive doesn't help. But this is where the boundaries you've put in place will be instrumental. Practicing self-control when you are tempted will strengthen your will and ability to resist temptation. As Christian partners, hold each other accountable in remaining pure and pursuing an honorable relationship.

Additionally, it is an indisputable reality that God calls us to remain pure before marriage, but what about the challenges of doing so after marriage? It's easy to put all the focus on purity during the premarital years and let it fall off the radar after marriage, but the reality is, Satan doesn't stop tempting you once you have a wedding

---

54 Charles Fain Lehman, "Fewer American High Schoolers Having Sex Than Ever Before," *Institute for Family Studies*, September 1, 2020, https://ifstudies.org/blog/fewer-american-high-schoolers-having-sex-than-ever-before.

55 "NSFG Listing P: Key Statistics from the National Survey of Family Growth," CDC, July 7, 2017, https://www.cdc.gov/nchs/nsfg/key_statistics/p.htm#premarital.

ring on your finger. He will try and try to make you fall until your last day. And remember, if your self-control is weak before marriage, it will stay weak after marriage, as St. John Chrysostom says in one of his homilies: "We must strive for self-control . . . St. Paul tells us to seek peace and satisfaction without which it is impossible to see the Lord. So whether we presently live in virginity, in our first marriage, or in our second, *let us pursue holiness*, that we may be counted worthy to see Him and to attain the Kingdom of Heaven."[56]

Finally, pursuing purity is also challenging because it is an ongoing journey that never ends.

* * * * *

Despite all the challenges, though, consider how beautiful it would be if our hearts became holy and purity left its footprint everywhere in our lives? And when you feel discouraged, remember that purity is born out of responding to God's call out of love and righteousness rather than out of fear, guilt, shame, or something else we've been conditioned to believe. Purity leads to freedom from immorality and the bond of sin, ultimately leading to holiness. "For God did not call us to be impure, but to live a holy life" (1 Thess. 4:7 [NIV]). Holiness is another word we often glance over, nod our heads to, and assume we know what it means. Some might feel like holiness is an unattainable standard reserved only for the saints. Others might feel like they have it under control, but in reality, they aim low and target the world's standards rather than the Bible's. The only way we can begin to understand the holiness we are called to is to get closer to the bearer of holiness Himself and familiarize ourselves with His Word.

---

56   Chrysostom, *On Marriage & Family Life,* 42.

In my own lifelong quest for purity, I've always found comfort in these words of His Holiness the late Pope Shenouda III, a highly revered leader in the Coptic Church, from his book *The Life of Repentance and Purity*. Perhaps you will find comfort in them too:

> Purity is the positive component in the life of repentance, the fruit of the change of life. In it disappears the desire for the world, the body, and sin; the desire of the heart becomes holy in the life of righteousness and the love of God . . . Purity covers your entire life, your expressions, senses, body, heart, and thoughts. You become a dwelling for the Holy Spirit from which the fruits of the Spirit appear.[57]

Myths about Purity

Myth # 1: No one stays pure, so I don't need to either.

Even if we see other people giving up on purity, that doesn't mean we should too! If the whole world is walking toward the fire, would you follow them? We have already seen throughout this chapter the consequences of doing so. And even though giving up on purity may seem like fun in the moment, if you examine the aftermath of people's sexually immoral actions, you'd most likely conclude that it does not lead to joy or fulfillment. It leaves them empty and searching for more. You, as a Christian, know that the only one who can fulfill all your desires is the Lord Himself, as the Psalmist says, "And I will delight myself in Your commandments, / Which I love" (Ps. 119:47). Nothing will satisfy our hearts more than delighting in the Lord.

---

57   Pope Shenouda III, *The Life of Repentance and Purity,* trans. Bishop Suriel (Yonkers, NY: St Vladimir's Seminary Press, 2016), 255.

The world might ridicule you for pursuing purity, as St. Anthony said, "A time is coming when men will go mad, and when they see someone who is not mad, they will attack him, saying, 'You are mad; you are not like us.'"[58] But remember, the world's judgment is not what matters: God will not judge you according to the standards of the world. He will hold you to *His* standards, perfectly outlined in Scripture. Saint Paul didn't say, "Flee sexual immorality as long as everyone else is doing so." He said, "Flee sexual immorality" (1 Cor. 6:18) and "Flee also youthful lusts; but pursue righteousness, faith, love, peace with those who call on the Lord out of a pure heart" (2 Tim. 2:22). The message is straightforward, although not necessarily easy to follow.

If the people around you question or challenge your commitment to purity, it might be a sign that you are not surrounding yourself with people who will support you in this journey. Find peers that value the same morals you do. Surround yourself with like-minded Christians who will encourage you to uphold the laws of the Lord. And have a group of people who will keep you accountable to do the right thing and remain pure.

Myth # 2: I will be rejected because of my lack of experience.

I've heard many young people express their frustration about this point: they meet someone who questions their choice to remain pure, arguing that their inexperience might result in physical or sexual frustration in the relationship. I typically challenge them and ask, "Well, if this person doesn't hold the same values of purity as

---

58   Benedicta Ward, *The Sayings of the Desert Fathers: The Alphabetical Collection,* vol. 59 (Collegeville, MN: Litugical Press, 1984), 6.

you do, do you think they're the right fit for you?" Purity should be a desired trait, not something that makes you undesirable. Your future spouse should honor and admire your purity because they honor the commands of God.

Purity should be something both people in the relationship strive toward, and they should uphold agreed-upon physical boundaries. There should not be pressure from one partner to push the other across a line they're not comfortable crossing. If someone is pressuring you or is not honoring your boundaries, this is a red flag. Let the pursuit of purity be a filter to eliminate someone who isn't right for you.

Myth # 3: If I remain pure, I'll be inexperienced for marriage.

That might be partly true, but it's a good problem to have. Sexual experience is not a prerequisite for a holy Christian marriage. God created men and women with perfectly compatible sexual organs, and when the time is right, together with your spouse you will figure out how to use them. Humans have figured it out for thousands of years, or reproduction would have stopped long ago, and we wouldn't be here. There's no need to practice or acquaint yourself with sexual experiences. There will be plenty of opportunities for that within the sacred bond of marriage.

As mentioned earlier in this chapter, a lack of self-control before marriage indicates a high chance of a lack of self-control after marriage—so don't make illegitimate excuses to satisfy your sexual curiosity. The devil will always present opportunities and temptations where you can explore sinful sexual desires before and after marriage. Remember that he is the enemy who wants to watch you fall. So be aware of who you're fighting against, "For we do not wrestle against flesh and blood, but against principalities, against powers, against the rulers of the darkness of this age, against spiritual hosts of wickedness in the heavenly places" (Eph. 6:12). Purity is an ongoing battle you must fight for a lifetime, and by the grace of God you will achieve victory.

8

Understanding God's Design for Sex

Michelle was a young woman who struggled to understand the purpose of sexuality and sex as God intended it. She grew up in a church where she was taught many negative ideas about sex along the lines of the problematic notions of purity discussed in the previous chapter. The ministry leaders in her church, although well-intentioned, warned of how destructive premarital sexual intercourse could be while neglecting to affirm the goodness and holiness of sex in the context of marriage. Over time, she began to associate sex with sin and shame. Even after she got married, she struggled with this idea.

Michelle could not understand how sex could be good—she could only see it as "wrong." It had been so ingrained in her that she wasn't allowed to enjoy or participate in sex that she avoided it altogether, which eventually caused her marriage to suffer. The issue became such a dividing wall in her marriage that she had to find help, and she sought counseling from a trustworthy priest, married mentors, and a therapist. Do you know what advice they gave her?

They told her to pray about the sexual union of her marriage. She should pray to God that she would enjoy the experience and for the comfort to know that God was happy that she was spending time with her husband in this way. The idea here was that, by inviting God into her experience through prayer, she might begin to associate sex with holiness in her marriage rather than shame.

Michelle began to understand that sex was one way she could have the intimacy and closeness she desired with her husband. Despite how strange it felt at first, over time, she began to truly enjoy the closeness achieved through this intimate time. This took years, because undoing a lifetime of thinking one way cannot happen overnight. But sure enough, she overcame her struggle through prayer, and the correct understanding of sex strengthened her marriage and faith.

This advice might not work for everyone struggling with the same shame around sex; therefore, everyone needs to seek their own counseling. But for Michelle, it was helpful because she came to understand that sex was not against the goodness of God and His creation, and that it is not sinful to desire your spouse in this way. Hebrews 13:4 says, "Marriage *is* honorable among all, and the bed undefiled; but fornicators and adulterers God will judge." We do not need to fear sex or our desire for it; rather, we need to maintain respect for it and understand how God intended it for marriage.

Whispers of Sex That Lead to Shame

Unfortunately, this is not just Michelle's story but also the story of quite a few other women I know. Similar situations existed in my church and home, as well as in the Orthodox homes and communities of many of my friends, regardless of their cultural, ethnic, or jurisdictional affiliations. At home, sex was rarely addressed positively or, frankly, at all. It only came up when it was unavoidable, like when inappropriate content played on TV in the presence of parents, who, in horror, changed the channel immediately—dismissing the subject altogether. Avoiding conversations about sex made it a taboo surrounded by impenetrable walls of shame.

I'm not shaming parents here. Many adults in the Orthodox communities I grew up in had made enormous transitions in immigrating to a new country. And so many of the taboos they inherited around sex were rooted in Middle Eastern cultural stigmas, often based in fear. Unfortunately, in many Middle Eastern or impoverished areas in developing countries, a girl's virginity is directly tied to her family's honor (not to mention their economic prospects). Premarital sex could mean being cast out and cut off from the entire community.

I grew up in several different parishes, and during my teenage years, I attended one that was proactive in discussing sex. There, the church leaders had noticed that we—the wide-eyed adolescent and teenage generation—were being swept away in a tornado of misinformation from the secular society surrounding us. Our gullible minds were exposed to too much too quickly, and our parents were not equipped to address the issue—so out of wisdom, the church stepped in like the mother we desperately needed. The church taught us about premarital sex and the physical and spiritual consequences it brought. While some of the teachings around purity were applied imperfectly at times, the intention was to help and benefit the youth, which it often did. Addressing it from a Christian perspective was more valuable than what society had to offer. But this was not the case in every Orthodox parish. (And I imagine you will find much of this discussion familiar, even if you grew up in other types of churches.)

Often, church leaders talk about sex mainly in one way—as forbidden fruit, only to be tasted in marriage, so you must avoid it at all costs while unmarried. It is a simplified message about abstinence that aligns with the biblical calling to flee sexual immorality, but that is it. No one talks about what happens on the other side of the line, the threshold you cross when you get married and become one flesh with someone else. Simply put, the conversations around sex in the church often stop at "Don't have sex until you're married; premarital sex is bad." To young minds, premarital sex becomes the only way sex is understood, which leads to the assumption that all sex is wrong.

Even if you receive this kind of message, like my friends and I, you probably can't help but wonder about the unspoken mystery, especially as you get older and closer to marriage. What should we expect from sex once we are married? How are we supposed to demonstrate Christian love through intimacy in marriage? What does a healthy Christian sex life look like? My friends and I only had a vague idea, and you may be in that situation too. These were all things I had to learn in my early years of marriage. Part of me wished that someone with more experience and wisdom would have addressed these questions with me because unanswered questions can lead to unrealistic expectations that put stress on marriages. Although I was vaguely aware that sex was a significant cause of marital problems, Orthodox resources that addressed it were few and far between.

In recent years, I've encountered more church leaders with professional psychology and marriage counseling qualifications who eloquently address this issue, so my hope for you is that you have experienced this, as all the issues I've been discussing in this chapter could be avoided if appropriately addressed at the right time. And that right time, believe it or not, is years before marriage. Our beliefs drive our expectations of what's to come, and our expectations drive our actions.

For church leaders, families, and individuals who have not yet done so, it's time to embark on a journey to understand God's intention for sex and manage our expectations around it. And that's what I hope this chapter will do for you. The journey begins with having personal and educated conversations with one another and addressing the topic of sex in order to destigmatize the taboo around it. Sex was created by God and is meant for the holiness of marriage, so let's address it as such.

I'm not saying the church needs to talk about sex in graphic detail, nor should you pursue this sort of discussion with church leaders. The birds and the bees talks should be reserved for conversations at home, where your parents can discern when and how much information they want you to know (or if you don't have parents around, a trusted family member or other adult who can do this for you). Unfortunately, these conversations don't always take place at home. Instead of participating in mature and informative discussions, young people may learn about sex from inappropriate sources, often being flooded with unverified information through pornography, the general media, or misinformed friends. There are endless sources that will infiltrate and corrupt our minds when they are young, and these may leave us curiously desiring what is sinful. Since what society teaches can be unhelpful to Christians, to adopt the correct view of sexuality let's go back to the beginning and try to understand God's intention for it.

In the Beginning

Have you ever wondered if purity and sexuality can harmoniously coexist? Or questioned where your sexual desires are coming from? Have you pondered what drives that innate attraction to the opposite sex? Or why you desire physical intimacy? There's a misconception that sexual desires are from the devil, yet the opposite is more in keeping with the Orthodox understanding of what it means to be human—our sexual desires were instilled initially within us by our Creator, God Himself. He purposely designed the gift of procreation and intimacy in marriage for our sake. It's a way to express our intangible love for someone in a tangible way, but when sin entered the world, that sexuality became a possible weapon Satan could use to lead us away from God.

When we understand God's design for our sexuality, we can better comprehend it, revere it, and see how good it is, just like everything God created. When God created the world, He created light, the firmament, dry ground, plants, the sun, the moon, the stars, the birds, the animals, and humanity—and deemed everything He made good. But then He stopped and proclaimed that something was *not* good. What was missing from His beautiful masterpiece? It was that man was alone: "And the LORD God said, '*It is* not good that man should be alone; I will make him a helper comparable to him'" (Gen. 2:18). Many like to refer to Eve as the crown of creation, and rightly so, as she was the last design of creation, making it complete. When Adam first laid eyes on Eve, he proclaimed: "This *is* now bone of my bones / And flesh of my flesh; / She shall be called Woman, / Because she was taken out of Man" (Gen. 2:23). Then Genesis continues: "Therefore a man shall leave his father and mother and be joined to his wife, and they shall become one flesh. And they were both naked, the man and his wife, and were not ashamed" (Gen. 2:24–25).

God created and initiated marriage and instructed Adam and Eve to procreate (note that this happened before the Fall). It was His idea to bring man and woman together and make them one flesh. One flesh in every sense of the word: spiritually, emotionally, and yes, physically. There was no shame in their nakedness and their union.

However, as sin enters the world through the enmity of the devil, before our very eyes, a drastic change occurs in Adam and Eve's relationship, which we see when God confronts Adam after he eats the forbidden fruit and shamefully hides. Adam says, "The woman whom You gave *to be* with me, she gave me of the tree, and I ate" (Gen. 3:12). Before the Fall, Adam marvels that Eve is part of his bone and flesh. He names her, and he sees her nakedness with no hint of shame. But after they sin, his tone takes a sharp turn. He blames God for giving Eve to him and claims she is the reason for his disobedience. The blame game is then born.

The birth of sin corrupted the marital relationship in other ways as well. When God first introduces His plan to create Eve, He says, "I will make him a *helper* [*ezer* in Hebrew, which means helpmate] comparable to him" (Gen. 2:18).[59] The word *ezer* appears twenty-one other times in the Old Testament, in all cases referring to God. In a worldly context, a helper is often considered someone less than the one they are helping, someone who cannot lead and always comes second. Yet that same word, *ezer*, describes God's strength, power, rescue, and protection throughout the Old Testament. Also, in the New Testament, the Holy Spirit is often called the Helper. So not only was Eve created in God's image but also according to His likeness as a helper. God had high regard for Eve and her role in the marital relationship, but as a consequence of the Fall, He told her, "Your desire *shall be* for your husband, / and he shall rule over you" (Gen. 3:16). This would lead to power struggles and a never-ending tug of war between wives and husbands. Sex became part of that

---

59   "Strong Concordance H5828 – Ezer," Blue Letter Bible, accessed January 16, 2022, https://www.blueletterbible.org/lexicon/h5828/nkjv/wlc/0-1/.

power struggle and has become a sore subject in many marriages, contributing to a lack of harmony. When the world took sex out of its original context, it corrupted what was meant to be a good gift.

What God Created and the World Corrupted

I can still smell the incense that filled the church on my wedding day. My husband and I were dressed like royalty—adorned with crowns and lavishly embroidered garments—as we stood before the holy altar of God and were anointed with holy oil. The traditions of the Coptic Orthodox wedding ceremony are symbolic. The husband and wife are united together, representing the relationship of Christ and the Church. Many visible symbols (e.g., crowns, holy oil, vestments) are used to portray the invisible mystery taking place as the Holy Spirit joins two separate individuals as one flesh.

As I stood there, experiencing a bit of stage fright, as all eyes were on me and my soon-to-be husband, I vividly remember the priest commanding us to submit to one another. He read the following: "So you too must know each other's rights and submit to one another. Let each of you be faithful toward the other, according to the saying of our teacher Paul the Apostle: 'The wife does not have authority over her own body, but the husband does. And likewise the husband does not have authority over his own body, but the wife does.'"[60]

Questions began flying around in my head. What did that even mean? How is it that I no longer have authority over my own body, but my husband does, and vice versa? What is this new authority I have over his body and he over mine?

---

[60] "Holy Matrimony - Crowning Ceremony. The Prayers Before the Altar," tasbeha.org, accessed April 18, 2023, https://tasbeha.org/hymn_library /view/1485.

I have come to learn that I was asking the wrong questions because I was still thinking in terms of me versus him. I thought we operated with our own interests in mind, often putting our own needs first, and I missed the mystery of us becoming one. When the sacrament is practiced to perfection, the will of both the husband and wife should unite in harmony, always seeking to please one another. We become one body and are not self-seeking or struggling for authority. This is a way we strive, in marriage, to overcome the rift between man and woman that occurred because of the Fall.

Yet today, we live in a hookup culture, where sex is a source of pleasure and self-gratification. It is also used as a weapon in a battle for power and control. Outside a pure marriage, sex may be exchanged for money or favors, it may be used to manipulate a person, or for selfish pleasure, along with many other evils. As professor and author Timothy O'Malley writes, "The narrative hookup culture tells us that love and sex are for sale, easily purchased and then left behind when new options present themselves. It forms us to see a separation between love and sex, between communion with another person and the pleasure we experience during sex."[61]

What God created as a beautiful, healing, binding, and bonding act within the holiness of marriage has been corrupted by sin—because of the Fall, yes, but also because of the way the world continues to operate. We live in a world that tells us to get what we want, that we're entitled to happiness, and where what we do with our body is considered our choice alone. These messages are everywhere you turn, directly or indirectly, and are often used to justify impure sexual relations.

However, we know from our Faith that we are meant to bond intimately with only the person we have become one flesh with, and

---

61   Timothy P. O'Malley, *Off the Hook: God, Love, Dating, and Marriage in a Hookup World* (Notre Dame, IN: Ave Maria Press, 2018), sec. "The Story of Hookup Culture."

if we crave that bond and satisfy it outside of marriage, it can become a losing spiritual battle. Although our loving God always offers a way back to the right path through forgiveness, it is not always an easy journey because we were made so that this special bond brings us physically and emotionally closer together. When oxytocin is released during sex it acts as a bonding chemical, bringing husband and wife closer together, not just physically, but emotionally as well. This natural occurrence is evidence of how God created the two to become one flesh in marriage. The feel-good feelings that come with sexual intercourse are God's way of allowing the male and female human body to enjoy an experience He created for good.

But secular society has normalized separating marriage and committed love from sex, even manipulating the meaning of love to fit an individual's agenda. The fact that someone can take that profoundly deep experience and water it down to a one-night stand, casual sex, or sex in exchange for money shows the brokenness of a society that has strayed away from the fear of God. In those cases, the emotional, mental, and spiritual intimacy of sex is removed and stripped down to just the physical act. Yet this act still has bonding effects. And if we allow ourselves to become bound to the wrong person, for the wrong reasons, or at the wrong time, it can become a massive hindrance that will take much time and effort to undo. For example, as I have mentioned earlier in this book, a physical bond can cause you to stay in an unhealthy or toxic relationship, fogging your logical reasoning. One partner can also become more attached to the other person, leading to an uneven emotional bond that is distressing and, worse, possibly addicting.[62]

---

62 Alessio Gori, Sara Russo, and Eleonora Topino, "Love Addiction, Adult Attachment Patterns and Self-Esteem: Testing for Mediation Using Path Analysis," *Journal of Personalized Medicine* 13, no. 2 (January 29, 2023): 247, https://doi.org/10.3390/jpm13020247.

Moreover, popular culture has made sex all about performance and satisfaction. With this, the component of self-sacrificial love in sexuality is replaced by satisfying one's sexual desires: it is no longer about the other person or the relationship but becomes about the self. And this is the opposite of how St. Paul describes love: "Love is patient, love is kind. It does not envy, it does not boast, it is not proud. It does not dishonor others, it is not self-seeking, it is not easily angered, it keeps no record of wrongs" (1 Cor. 13:4–6 [NIV]). Sex can be one of the places in the marriage where each spouse practices putting their partner's needs before their own, a true act of self-sacrifice.

Dangers of "Sexpectations"

Our preconceived notions about sex, especially if they have been influenced by secular culture, can lead to unrealistic expectations. I once was invited to present a talk at a retreat for college youth about different types of relationships. I focused the discussion on the foundational relationships in our life—our ties to God, family, friends, and significant others. I knew the audience would be most interested in the last one because thinking about and searching for romantic relationships during the college years can sometimes feel consuming. I saved some time at the end for anonymous questions to be submitted, and one question read, "Is oral sex okay?" Since no one in the audience was married, I assumed they were talking about oral sex during the dating phase, and obviously, the answer was no. I spent some time discussing how we need to pursue purity, not just worry about crossing the line of intercourse.

After I finished speaking, a young unmarried man approached my husband and me to clarify that he sent the question and meant to ask about it in the context of marriage. He was eager to find out the Church's stance on it. "Why?" I asked, and he explained that he and his friends often talked about it, and he hinted that it was something they wanted to experience in marriage. Although his question was fair to ask, the intention behind it was a little worrisome because these curious young men were spending a lot of time and energy building up their expectations about sex before marriage. This is risky because during marriage such "sexpectations" often lead to pressure, arguments, and disappointment over unmet expectations.

Building expectations like this is also not helpful because when we think about all we want to do after marriage, we usually think about ourselves, *our* pleasure, *our* satisfaction, and typically not the needs of our future spouse. But Christian love is all about sacrifice and giving yourself to the other person, and indeed, "it is more blessed to give than to receive" (Acts 20:35). Sexual pleasure is often a result of giving ourselves to another, but it shouldn't be our main focus.

In fact, it is dangerous to place sex at the forefront of our thinking. In their book *Two Become One,* Fr. Antonios Kaldas and Ireni Attia write:

> Sex plays a much bigger role than it deserves and occupies an unhealthy, disproportionately large place in our thinking. When sex acquires this over-importance, it begins to be dangerous, and Paradise is lost. Sex then no longer leads to the unselfish self-sacrifice and self-giving which is the image of God. Instead it leads to addiction, enslavement by the passions, and a focus on satisfying one's own desires, even at the cost of others, as an overriding motivation in life.[63]

---

63 Antonios Kaldas and Ireni Attia, *Two Become One: An Orthodox Christian Guide to Engagement and Marriage* (Chesterton, IN: Ancient Faith Publishing, 2017), 166.

The authors continue, "Sexuality is good if it is used the right way, as a means to growing in divine love. But if it is abused, it becomes not a blessing but a curse in our lives, corrupting us and spoiling the image of the God of love in us." I would heed their warning and work on developing the correct Christian mentality about sexuality in marriage—even before you are married.

What you shouldn't do before you are married, though, is explicitly discuss your sexual fantasies with your partner, because this could bring on temptation. I recommend that you talk to trustworthy married mentors about any sexual questions you both have and even about what to expect. This can also be something to discuss with a counselor if you are doing premarital counseling (which I highly recommend for every couple). Your mentors or counselor should be able to help you set healthy expectations so that you don't enter marriage with ones that will prove to be unhelpful. Rather, it would be more helpful to talk about your views of sex and sexuality and making sure those align with one another, as well as with God's design for it.

There is no need to go into great detail about your sexual expectations, as those will become more clear after you are married. If there is something to discuss in detail, it would be what you expect for the wedding night as the time gets closer to it. I have heard of couples not wanting to be intimate on the wedding night and instead waiting for when they are well-rested, while some just want to jump right in. If you're planning on the former, it's a good idea to bring it up with your partner, who might be expecting the latter. Some even choose an older, rare practice of spending three days praying and fasting at a monastery before consummating their marriage. Something like that requires clear communication and planning.

After that night, when you are now one flesh, you are free and highly encouraged to discuss your expectations while accepting that compromise might be needed to reach a mutual agreement. This is not just a conversation you have once but one to discuss throughout your marriage. As you grow together, so do your desires, likes, and dislikes, so make sure you openly communicate that to your spouse and do not leave them to guess. Ask how you can please one another in every area of the marriage, not just sexually. Pray that God will allow your marriage bond to be strengthened and solidified through intimacy and to use it as a path to sanctification.

Having God as the center of your relationship is sure to bless your marriage and leave you satisfied with it. In fact, religious married couples who attend church services together have reported high satisfaction with their sexual relationship and a higher frequency of having sex. About three-quarters of these couples have reported that they are very happy with their sexual relationship compared to those who are not churchgoers.[64]

Myths about Sex

Myth #1: If I save myself for marriage, my sex life will automatically be wonderful.

Chloe and Zack were faithful Christians who dated for a while before marriage. Although they were tempted on many occasions to cross the boundary they had set for their physical relationship, they waited until marriage to have sex. But once it was the right time to be physically intimate, they found that it did not meet their expectations. They thought that because they had waited and obeyed God's commandments around purity, He would instantly reward them with a great sex life. They were disappointed when their intimacy

---

64 W. Bradford Wilcox and Wendy Wang, "Sacred Sex," *First Things*, February 15, 2024, https://www.firstthings.com/web-exclusives/2024/02/sacred-sex.

with one another didn't live up to the intimate scenes they saw on their electronic screens and had stored in their minds over the years.

But here's the thing: nowhere in the Bible is an amazing sex life promised as a reward for waiting until marriage. Rather, the goal of marriage is salvation, which is different than earthly pleasure. A couple's sex life will not be instantly wonderful simply because they made the right decision to stay pure. It's just that by doing so, they avoid certain difficulties and struggles that result from sexual immorality. In the purity movement that followed in the wake of the book *I Kissed Dating Goodbye*, the false promise of amazing sex during marriage was used almost as a bargaining chip to convince youth to remain pure. At other times, it was used as a scare tactic, as though a couple's sex life would be deficient if they didn't remain pure before marriage. Yet commands for purity and chastity are not things we obey because of a future reward or punishment. Purity and chastity are things we pursue because we are called to do so as Christians. It's not for anyone else but for honoring and obeying God.

At the same time, there is no denying the correlation between virginity and a happy marital sex life. A study done at the Institute for Family Studies found that "Americans who have only ever slept with their spouses are most likely to report being in a 'very happy' marriage." And W. Bradford Wilcox, a sociologist and senior fellow at the Institute for Family Studies stated, "Contrary to conventional wisdom, when it comes to sex, less experience is better, at least for the marriage."[65]

Why would people like Chloe and Zack struggle with their sex life when they are first married, then? Because a great sex life takes time and work. Sometimes it can even take months or years for

---

65   Olga Khazan, "Fewer Sex Partners Means a Happier Marriage" *The Atlantic*, October 22, 2018, https://www.theatlantic.com/health/archive/2018/10/sexual-partners-and-marital-happiness/573493/.

spouses to cultivate an enjoyable and holy sex life. And having a great physical connection isn't just about the physical act, but emotional and spiritual connection as well. Honoring each other and putting a spouse's needs first can be challenging. Constantly sacrificing for another person does not come naturally in marriage; rather, it has to be done intentionally. But all the work is worth it when a married couple arrives at a place where they find fulfillment in one another. It truly is a remarkable gift from God. But keep in mind that sex is not the end-all and be-all of marriage. It is just one part of it, serving the purpose of procreation and of further solidifying the marital bond. There are also many other beautiful aspects of marriage.

Myth #2: Sexual compatibility is important to figure out before marriage.

Actually, biological sexual compatibility is easy to figure out. If one partner is male and the other is female, then by nature and God's design, their sexual organs are compatible. Add to that the physical attraction they have for one another, and you arrive at sexually compatibility. This might be an oversimplification of an intricate matter, but it's not as highly complex as some make it out to be. When people refer to sexual compatibility, they mean the "try it before you buy it" mentality, which refers to sleeping with a partner to test sexual satisfaction. If we know what sex is really about, we won't believe this lie. Sex isn't just about pleasure and satisfaction; that's just one part of it. It's not something to test and see if it would be a deal-breaker. You'd be placing a disproportionate weight on the external action. When checking for compatibility, there are much weightier internal matters to consider.

When the Holy Spirit unites two people as one flesh, sexual satisfaction will eventually follow, though it might take time and might be more challenging for some than others. Welcome to one of the many struggles of marriage. It takes time for each spouse to adjust to one another after marriage. No one becomes an expert in sex overnight. It takes time and patience, so go into marriage with the expectation that this is a journey to go on together.

Don't buy into the false idea society is trying to sell. When people argue, "You have to try it before you buy it," they are comparing premarital sex to test driving a car before purchasing it. Are we really comparing a spouse to a car? The primary function of a car is to carry out our own need for getting from one destination to another. Yet our spouse offers way more than the simple notion of satisfying our sexual needs. They challenge us for our betterment and sanctification in order to help us reach salvation. They are more than a body at our disposal, like a car is. The marital relationship is about more than just sex.

Myth #3: Sex will be exactly like what I see in the media.

Is anything we see in the media an accurate depiction of real life? Most likely not! I hope you are not deceived by TV shows, movies, or even porn, or you will be disappointed in real life. Sex scenes in the entertainment industry are staged, acted out, and choreographed to make you feel a certain way. A crew of actors, directors, and other team members work for days and spend thousands (if not millions) of dollars to produce this type of entertainment. It is simply not the real thing. The goal is to get you hooked on the dopamine hit your brain experiences as you watch sexual content, so you continually return for more. Not only do these scenes mess with your brain chemicals, they also distort reality and build false expectations around sex.

The good news is that sex is not like what you see in the movies; it can be even better if done with the right spirit of honor and love because as we've seen in this book, good sex isn't just physical: it builds intimacy and connection. Romantic intimacy solidifies the emotional bond that brings you closer to your partner. Sex is a beautiful gift in a marriage to deepen the love a husband and wife have for one another, as St. John Chrysostom said, "Sex is not evil, it is a gift from God."[66]

---

66 Grube, *What the Church Fathers Say About . . .* , 65.

9

Fighting Temptation

Sometimes we find ourselves at a crossroads where we have to choose between controlling our sinful desires or fulfilling them. Sin is typically attractive and enticing, or we wouldn't even be tempted to give in to it. It lights up the pleasure center in our brain and makes us feel good instantly, but also just momentarily. Yet, when we know the right choice and choose the opposite, we willingly indulge in sin. We are not alone in having to deal with this dilemma—even Paul the apostle questions his actions when he admits, "For what I am doing, I do not understand. For what I will to do, that I do not practice; but what I hate, that I do" (Rom. 7:15). He then concludes, "If, then, I do what I will not to do, I agree with the law that *it is* good. But now, *it is* no longer I who do it, but sin that dwells in me" (vv. 16–17).

Saint Paul knew, though, that while sin dwells in all of us, we do not have to let it control us: we are free and able to overcome sin by the grace offered by our Savior. The Church Father St. Augustine helps us understand this when he comments on the above Scripture verses, saying, "The man being described here is under the law, before the coming of grace. Sin overpowers him when he attempts to live righteously in his own strength, without the help of God's liberating grace."[67] Saint Augustine knew all about this, because he was a man who, for many years, chased his desires and gave in to the temptation to sin. It wasn't until he sought the one true God that he began to live a life in repentance. It was God's liberating grace that brought him into a new life.

Temptation comes in many forms when you're single or dating because your pursuit of purity infuriates the enemy of our souls. Satan doesn't want you to see yourself as a child of a God, who will fulfill the desires of your heart; rather, he wants you to see others as the means to fulfilling your desires. But there are ways to recognize these temptations, understand their effects on you, and fight back. This chapter will walk you through this process. Let's first address one of the biggest temptations plaguing teens and young adults—the silent killer of purity and chastity: pornography.

The Temptation Industry

There are many sinful things that the Western world has normalized that are clearly against God's commands, including one-night stands, cohabitation before marriage, and having multiple sexual partners. But one of the major things you'll encounter is the temptation to use porn, as the advent of the internet has given everyone easy access to it. What used to be found only in magazines and

---

67 Gerald Bray, *Romans: Ancient Christian Commentary on Scripture,* NT vol. 6 (Downers Grove, IL: InterVarsity Press, 1999), 186.

videos that you had to purchase in person is now easily accessible to anyone with an electronic device and internet service.

In 2014, the global porn industry was estimated to be a $97 billion industry worldwide, with $10–$12 billion coming from the United States.[68] It was reported that in 2017 there were 28.5 billion annual visits to porn sites, which is a staggering 81 million visits daily, on average.[69] Covenant Eyes, an anti-porn software created by Christians to help porn users overcome their addiction, has provided research on porn use, and here are just some of their findings:[70] 28,258 users are watching pornography every second, with $3,075.64 being spent per second on porn online. The average age of exposure to pornography for men is twelve years old. Porn use has become so normalized that when talking to friends, 90 percent of teens and 96 percent of young adults are encouraging, accepting, or neutral about it. And 45 percent of adults twenty-five and older don't believe that watching porn is wrong. And all this is not just a problem for non-Christians: 64 percent of Christian men and 15 percent of Christian women say they watch porn at least once a month.

These statistics might seem like only numbers, but those numbers represent people, and they reflect the sad reality that many people don't know the full extent of the effect that watching porn has on them. Many think it's not harming anyone, including themselves,

---

68   "Things Are Looking Up in America's Porn Industry," *NBC News*, updated January 20, 2015, https://www.nbcnews.com/business/business-news/things -are-looking-americas-porn-industry-n289431.

69   "The Most Viewed Porn Categories Of 2017 Are Pretty Messed Up," Fight the New Drug, accessed February 24, 2023, https://fightthenewdrug.org /pornhub-reports-most-viewed-porn-of-2017/.

70   "Pornography Statistics," Covenant Eyes, January 3, 2022, https://www .covenanteyes.com/pornstats/.

but the findings of numerous studies tell a different story.[71] A study done with male participants found that watching pornography is associated with both animalistic and mechanistic dehumanization.[72] Animalistic dehumanization is perceiving another human as closer to an animal incapable of complex emotions or thinking, while mechanistic dehumanization views humans as objects. Both forms of dehumanization lead to denying that others possess human qualities, personality, emotions, or individuality, which denies them human dignity.[73]

Another damaging ramification is the sexual objectification of women, which is a common theme found throughout porn. This leads to sexually aggressive attitudes and behaviors in men, which unfortunately isn't surprising, as another study found that 88 percent of pornographic scenes contained physical aggression, and nearly half (48 percent) contained verbal aggression toward women. In those scenes, women were depicted responding either neutrally or positively.[74]

Violence and aggression aren't the only effects of porn use; it also influences one's ability to become sexually aroused by normal sexual contact. One study found an association between sexual dysfunction for both men and women with problematic pornography

---

71 See numerous studies at Truth About Porn, https://truthaboutporn.org /study.

72 Yanyan Zhou et al., "Pornography Use, Two Forms of Dehumanization, and Sexual Aggression: Attitudes vs. Behaviors," *Journal of Sex & Marital Therapy* 47, no. 6 (May 14, 2021): 571–90, https://doi.org/10.1080/00926 23x.2021.1923598.

73 Kalina Christoff, "Dehumanization in Organizational Settings: Some Scientific and Ethical Considerations," *Frontiers in Human Neuroscience* 8 (September 24, 2014), https://doi.org/10.3389/fnhum.2014.00748.

74 Ana Bridges et al., "Aggression and Sexual Behavior in Best-selling Pornography Videos: A Content Analysis Update," *Violence Against Women* 16, no. 10 (October 26, 2010): 1065–85, https://doi. org/10.1177/1077801210382866.

consumption.[75] One story I heard when I was in high school illustrates this issue. I attended a public high school where teachers casually taught the practice of safe sex in health class, and I'll never forget one presentation in particular.

In this class session, a guest speaker delivered a presentation that didn't focus on safe sex but on abstinence instead. Not everyone received her message well, but I listened with open ears. She started her presentation by talking about the objectification of women in advertisements, mainstream media, and pornography. She then told us the story of a young man she knew who had been a frequent user of porn. He was saving sex for marriage, ironically thinking that drawing the line there meant he was doing the right thing—but to his surprise and the disappointment of his bride, on his wedding night, he found himself unable to have sex. His wife, a beautiful woman, couldn't compare to the porn actresses he was used to; therefore, he could not become sexually aroused. He spent most of his night alone in the hotel lobby while his wife was heartbroken about what had become of their special night. As this story illustrates, porn robs you of the ability to experience the joy of real sex because it rewires your brain and alters what you find attractive. It is choreographed to portray a fantasy, and the people involved usually have artificial and unrealistic bodies.

Another danger of porn use—and a reason why it is highly tempting—is that it is easy to get addicted to it. In fact, scientists are calling porn "the new drug" due to its highly addictive nature. When you watch porn, a number of hormones and neurotransmitters are released, such as dopamine, norepinephrine, oxytocin,

---

75   Báta Bőthe et al., "Are Sexual Functioning Problems Associated with Frequent Pornography Use and/or Problematic Pornography Use? Results from a Large Community Survey Including Males and Females," *Addictive Behaviors* 112 (August 15, 2020): 106603, https://doi.org/10.1016/j.addbeh.2020.106603.

endorphins, and serotonin.[76] These chemicals were designed for release during real sexual intercourse, but porn tricks the body into believing it is experiencing the real thing. The more you watch porn, the more you flood yourself with these chemicals and program your body to be aroused by specific images. Then, unfortunately, when it's time for the real thing with a real person—the spouse you chose—reality doesn't live up to the expectations you've accustomed yourself to.

The other stumbling block associated with pornography is that it often leads to masturbation. The implications of masturbation are not just physical but spiritual as well. Masturbation is problematic because it is often triggered by lustful thoughts, and we know what our Lord Jesus Christ said about that in the gospels: if we look at someone in a lustful way, we've committed adultery (Matt. 5:28). It follows that if someone masturbates, they are typically thinking or looking at something sexually provocative, and this is sinful. Although thinking about sex in a healthy and mature manner isn't a sin, entertaining lustful sexual desires is. So be aware of your thoughts and bring "every thought into captivity to the obedience of Christ" (2 Cor. 10:5).

Masturbation is considered sinful as it "misses the mark" of what real sex was meant for.[77] It mimics the physical pleasure of sex, but pleasure is not the main goal of sex—it is meant to build a deeper union between husband and wife, and it is meant for procreation.

---

76 Luke Gilkerson, "Brain Chemicals and Porn: How Porn Affects Your Brain," Covenant Eyes, updated March 1, 2024, https://www.covenant eyes.com/blog/brain-chemicals-and-porn-addiction/.

77 "Church's View of Masturbation," Orthodox Church in America, accessed April 26, 2024, https://www.oca.org/questions/dailylife/churchs-view-of -masturbation.

Masturbation is only self-serving as it does not carry out the goodness and fruit of sex intended by God.

It's important to understand why some are drawn to porn use and the root behind it. Many men and women think that their sex drive causes porn to be tempting to them, but the issue is much more complex than that. In fact, some psychologists and therapists have found that what leads someone to watch porn is not necessarily the entertainment aspect or the lure of sexual gratification; rather, it's more about connection. Humans naturally long for intimacy—not just physical, but emotional and relational intimacy too—and when they feel isolated and without real human connection, loneliness starts creeping in. For many, the easiest way to escape the feeling of loneliness is to turn to porn. But instead of solving the problem of loneliness, porn actually creates more of it. Mark Butler, a professor and marriage and family therapist, writes, "If loneliness can lead to pornography use, and pornography use may bring about or intensify loneliness, these circular linkages may create a vicious cycle, pulling the user even further from health-promoting relationship connections."[78]

These problems don't exist only with explicit porn use. Andrew Williams writes in his book, *From Object to Icon: The Struggle for Spiritual Vision in a Pornographic World*, "Even those of us who might think we don't have any connection with pornography need to take a closer look. Our modern globalized society has increasingly 'pornified' its media and advertising."[79] Unfortunately, many

---

78 Mark Butler, "Is Pornography Use Increasing Loneliness, Particularly for Young People?" Institute for Family Studies, July 3, 2018, https://ifstudies .org/blog/is-pornography-use-increasing-loneliness-particularly-for-young -people.

79 Andrew Williams, introduction to *From Object to Icon: The Struggle for Spiritual Vision in a Pornographic World* (Chesterton, IN: Ancient Faith Publishing, 2023).

TV and streaming shows are filled with nude scenes that are easily accessible to anyone of any age, regardless of the TV rating. Even in literature, romance novels that depict erotic sexual scenes are another form of pornography. While it may be under the disguise of reading, an intellectual pastime, its intent is to sexually arouse the reader, making for a more "enjoyable" reading experience. It may not be porn accessed online, but if any content is leading you to have sexual thoughts, fantasies, desires, or if it arouses you, then its effects become similar to porn. In all cases, you must address the issue before it becomes a problem that consumes you.

Remember that getting married is not the answer to solving your lust or porn use problem. In fact, marriage takes any problem you have and magnifies it, because it is no longer just about you but your spouse also. You must overcome the problem before you enter marriage, and your partner should be aware of your struggle, as keeping that a secret could be a detriment to the success of your marriage. Recognizing the temptation, setting a plan for avoiding it, and practicing self-control are all key ways to overcome sexual temptations. The rest of this chapter will give you advice about how to do these things, but if you suspect you have developed a sexual addiction, it's time to seek the help of a professional counselor.

Recognize the Temptation

My kids know that Monday nights are special for our family: we often go out to eat and squeeze in some fun activity. One Monday night, we went to a restaurant near New York City that we had never been to before. It seemed like a family restaurant, with no bar in sight and food for all ages. We arrived early before the dinner rush, secured a corner table, and eagerly awaited our food.

All around the restaurant, TVs were up like wallpaper borders on the walls, without an inch of space between them, and as people trickled in someone turned them on. Suddenly, nonstop music videos of half-naked men and women dancing provocatively to explicit lyrics filled the restaurant. It seemed that, apart from my husband and I, everyone else was unbothered by this. Luckily our girls were young toddlers at the time and didn't pay much attention to the TVs playing in the background. We asked the waitstaff to turn off the TVs by our table, but that didn't stop us from seeing and hearing the other TVs in the large dining room. We ate quickly, fed the kids, and got out of there as fast as possible.

When you find yourself in a circumstance like the one I described above, it's important to assess the situation: you should know your limits and what you can handle versus what will lead you to temptation. Had I been in that situation in my younger years, I would have probably not been able to handle all the lustful thoughts that would have intruded from watching and hearing what was playing on those TVs.

There is no shame in getting up and leaving a room that is too tempting for you. In fact, research has proven that the environment you're in makes a significant difference in avoiding a temptation. A study of Vietnam War veterans referenced in the bestselling book *Atomic Habits* found that 20 percent of US soldiers stationed in Vietnam were addicted to heroin. They had easy access to it, were surrounded by fellow soldiers who used it, and it provided a way to escape the stress of war. But approximately nine out of ten of those soldiers eliminated their addiction when they came back home. A similar phenomenon happens when a drug addict goes to a rehab center. When an addict is no longer surrounded by their typical environment and cues that trigger the drug use, they can get clean.

Yet 90 percent of heroin users become addicted again once they return to their usual environment at home.[80]

This study proves the power of environment and how it is a key factor in overcoming unwanted behaviors. So instead of just relying on self-control and resisting temptations, set yourself up for success by being in the right environment, as James Clear writes, "People with high self-control tend to spend less time in tempting situations. It's easier to avoid temptation than resist it."[81] As time goes on and you grow to conquer the temptation, you might be able to face it without it affecting you. But in the meantime, control your environment to help control your temptations.

As you practice resisting temptation you will grow stronger in fighting it, or ideally get rid of it all together. I once heard a story about a young man who accompanied a Coptic Orthodox bishop to the mall. The bishop was visiting from another country and wanted to buy some goods not available where he was from. As they walked through the mall, they walked in front of a Victoria's Secret store. If you've ever been in an American mall, you know that Victoria's Secret storefronts present half-naked supermodels advertising female undergarments in seductive and alluring photos. While the young man tried to walk past it quickly, gazing the other way awkwardly, the bishop looked at the advertisements and said, "Wow, those women are really healthy." This bishop was not bothered by any lustful thoughts that might accompany those images because he had overcome that temptation and could see them plainly as women.

This story shows how different people will have different reactions to a possible temptation in their environment: for one it will

---

80   James Clear, *Atomic Habits: An Easy & Proven Way to Build Good Habits & Break Bad Ones* (New York, NY: Penguin Random House, 2018), 91–92.

81   Clear, 95.

be a stumbling block, and for the other it won't lead to intrusive thoughts. You have to know which one you tend to be like when in a similar situation and what your internal reaction will be like. When you can identify your triggers for temptation, you have a greater chance of coming up with a good defense plan.

Guard Your Senses

Being on guard in a world full of temptations can feel like a constant battle, but there are ways to set ourselves up for success and make these struggles feel less daunting. The enemy, knowing our weaknesses, tries to use our surroundings and our senses to lead us into temptation. But the good news is that those are all things we have control over. The wise advice found in Proverbs 4 can help equip us for the battles we face in today's world where many sinful things have become the norm:

> Keep your heart with all diligence,
> For out of it *spring* the issues of life.
> Put away from you a deceitful mouth,
> And put perverse lips far from you.
> Let your eyes look straight ahead,
> And your eyelids look right before you.
> Ponder the path of your feet,
> And let all your ways be established.
> Do not turn to the right or the left;
> Remove your foot from evil. (vv. 23–27)

These verses tell us to guard our hearts by protecting our senses. Our mouths, eyes, ears, and feet must comply with the instruction of the Lord and walk in righteousness.

Guard Your Mouth

When I was in middle school, each class was assigned to a large table for lunchtime. While this eliminated the dreaded rejection for the less popular kids in school, it also removed any choice you had over who to sit with, so sometimes I would end up seated with students whose conversations made me uncomfortable. Middle school is a time when many search for their identity as they hit puberty and try to navigate the changes that come with it. Most of the guys in my class tried to show their masculinity by exchanging perverted jokes and stories. Not overhearing these conversations was hard, and if you wanted to seem cool and fit in, you joined them.

What these students probably didn't realize was that our words are powerful; they can lead our minds to pureness or perverseness. Our mouth exposes the true motives of our heart, and the words we speak reflect our internal thoughts, like Luke 6:45 says: "A good man out of the good treasure of his heart brings forth good. . . . For out of the abundance of the heart his mouth speaks." If we surround ourselves with people whose hearts are far from God, we start resembling their condition, and soon our words begin to match theirs. To try to combat this, during middle school lunchtime I would move to the opposite side of the table and try to initiate different conversations than the ones I overheard. Not laughing at the perverted jokes protected me and also sent a message to those making them—that I wouldn't participate in their inappropriate conversations. Eventually, as I graduated to high school, I was able to choose the friends I wanted to have lunch with. It made a world of a difference having like-minded Christian friends who wanted to have godly conversations rather than inappropriate ones.

So in order to guard your mouth, you need to align your words with your heart. Examine the words proceeding from your mouth and question how they got there. And guard your ears, because that will help you guard your mouth: the music you listen to, the conversations you hear, and the media you consume will all affect your thoughts and ultimately your words. If catchy vulgar lyrics linger in your mind after hearing a song, they will taint your thoughts and, eventually, influence your desires. If you listen to the world's truth, it will slowly overshadow God's truth and take over your belief system. We repeat the things we hear and start to believe them.

Guard Your Eyes and Ears

The gift of eyesight opens us to the world and all its beauty but also its temptations, and with today's technology, you can see anyone and anything, anywhere, anytime. Nothing is off limits on the internet: modern men can see more naked women than King Solomon did with his hundreds of wives and concubines. Both men and women can access images and videos of thousands, if not millions, of women and men online. But while the world offers to satisfy your sexual curiosity by giving you access to endless images and videos, these will infiltrate your pure mind, and your curiosity will grow. So don't entertain any images you know are ungodly, not even for a split second. And don't underestimate the strength of your memory when it comes to storing these images. An image viewed for seconds can last in our memory way beyond those few seconds—for twelve years to be exact.

A study was done to test the power of explicit memory (conscious long-term memory). It revealed that participants were able to recognize drawings shown to them for two seconds on average, either once or three times, approximately twelve years earlier.[82] Another study done by a team of neuroscientists from MIT found that the

---

82   Christelle Larzabal et al., "Extremely Long-Term Memory and Familiarity after 12 Years," *Cognition* 170 (January 2018): 254–62, https://doi.org/10 .1016/j.cognition.2017.10.009.

human brain can process entire images that the eye sees for as little as thirteen milliseconds.[83] If you're unfamiliar with that time measurement, there are one thousand milliseconds in one second, so your mind can register images in just a tiny fraction of a second.

Your memory has great power to recognize images, whether good or bad, and whether you see them voluntarily or involuntarily. Guard your eyes so they may not see things that will defile your heart and tempt your will. Christ even goes as far as to tell us to pluck out our eye if it is the source of our stumbling. "If your right eye causes you to sin, pluck it out and cast *it* from you; for it is more profitable for you that one of your members perish, than for your whole body to be cast into hell" (Matt. 5:29). He cares the most for your salvation, and He doesn't want the weakness of your senses to rob you of the glory He has waiting for you. It's time to eliminate whatever is hindering your purity and causing you to sin.

To best guard your eyes, examine all the things you see, no matter how trivial you think they might be. Are the shows and movies you watch filled with edifying content or things that contribute to ungodly thoughts and desires? If you have social media, what kinds of people and pages are you following? Are you finding that your social media news feed brings you informative and edifying content, or does it trap you in sin? When you find yourself in unavoidable public places with temptation lurking around, what are you fixing your eyes on and what thoughts are initiated? Remember that your eyes are the gatekeepers of what enters your body, as it says in Matthew 6:22–23: "The lamp of the body is the eye. If therefore your eye is good, your whole body will be full of light. But if your

---

83   Anne Trafton, "In the Blink of an Eye," MIT News, January 16, 2014, https://news.mit.edu/2014/in-the-blink-of-an-eye-0116.

eye is bad, your whole body will be full of darkness. If therefore the light that is in you is darkness, how great *is* that darkness!"

Guard Your Feet

In the Proverbs passage at the start of this section, two verses are dedicated to telling us about the importance of being careful with our steps. Our feet can take us to places known for being filled with temptation, or they can lead us away from those places. Avoiding places of temptation is a large part of the battle. Skipping out on parties notorious for drinking and promiscuity is a safe way to avoid temptation, and not stepping foot in certain entertainment clubs will protect your purity.

Joseph and David were two men in the Old Testament who faced sexual temptation. One man's feet led him to freedom, and the other's led to his downfall. When Potiphar's wife cornered Joseph because she desired him, he refused to sin (Gen. 39:7–20). Quick on his feet (literally), he fled from temptation and ran outside, leaving his garments in her hands—which was just enough evidence to frame him for a crime. He was wrongfully imprisoned for honoring God's way and resisting temptation, but eventually he was rewarded for his faithfulness by becoming a prominent leader in Egypt. Had he not moved his feet and instead allowed himself to fall into temptation, Joseph's story would be a different one.

On the other hand, David's feet led to his compromise (2 Sam. 11). When his feet were at home idling instead of being at battle as kings normally would be during that time of year, his steps led him to the roof of his palace where he saw Bathsheba, a beautiful woman, bathing on her rooftop. Instead of walking away immediately, he stood still and his heart desired her. He walked back inside to inquire about her and had his servant bring her to him. Walking into his chambers with her, his feet led him to the bed where he would commit adultery, which caused God to later reproach him. And because sin usually entangles us and leads to more sin, David found himself facilitating her husband's death in order to try to cover up his initial mistake.

So like Joseph, be aware of where your feet take you; control the steps they pursue. Let your feet be the beautiful feet that bring glad tidings and the gospel of peace to others (Rom. 10:15). Where your feet walk, the rest of your body and senses will follow, so let them lead you to walk in righteousness.

Count the Cost

If we forgo guarding our senses and don't deliberately fight temptation, we can find ourselves being led by our desires. Our desires can be a double-edged sword. If good they will lead us to holiness, but if tainted by sin they will lead to our downfall. Following our ungodly desires will leave us acting on impulse or emotion, which comes with a cost that may not be worth it. We see this with the story of Esau, who did not count the cost before he gave up something of great value.

One day Esau came home weary and famished. He claimed to be hungry to the point of death and begged his brother Jacob for food (Gen. 25:29–34). Jacob probably expected Esau would arrive home weak and hungry from his labor, so he had cooked a savory meal knowing it would entice Esau, and he asked Esau for his birthright in exchange for it. As the eldest son, Esau would have received twice Jacob's inheritance and would be the male in charge of family affairs in their father's absence and after his passing.

When Jacob asked to buy his older brother's birthright, Esau exclaimed, "Look, I *am* about to die; so what *is* this birthright to me?" (Gen. 25:32)—and instead of counting the cost, he sold his birthright for a stew of lentils and bread that day. All Esau cared about at that moment was satisfying the hunger and pain his flesh felt. His hunger clouded his judgment, and he could not see past this feeling.

Many of us find ourselves in the same predicament; blinded by our intense desires, we lose sight of the consequences they can bear. Saint Paul warns against such actions when he writes, "lest there *be* any fornicator or profane person like Esau, who for one morsel of food sold his birthright" (Heb. 12:16). Esau's fornication was his unfaithfulness to God, which is the choice we make every time we follow our desires and sin against God.

So count your costs before entering the battle that awaits you daily. The battle with fulfilling the lust of the flesh and indulging in your desires will always be there. Is momentary satisfaction worth the consequences? Is a short-term, physically intimate relationship worth the long-term issues that will follow? Is sending explicit pictures to someone worth your tainted reputation when it gets out? Is complying with your partner's sexual desires worth compromising your purity?

The simple answer to all these questions is no; none of these situations are worth it. But in a moment of weakness, giving into temptation might mistakenly seem worth it, and the devil will try to convince you it isn't a big deal, that your desires are worth attending to. He wants you to believe that satisfying your flesh has no real consequences. But when you find yourself in that place, remember that you are not his weak prey, but you can mightily fight back and win the battle.

Fight Back

Saint Peter warns us to "be sober, be vigilant; because your adversary the devil walks about like a roaring lion, seeking whom he may devour" (1 Pet. 5:8). He was no stranger to the devil's sharp teeth, having given in to the temptation to deny Christ, not once but three times. Saint Peter could have stopped there and not sought repentance afterward, but he chose to fight back and turn from his ways as soon as he heard the rooster crow.

Fighting sexual immorality or any other sin is no easy battle, but St. Dorotheus of Gaza writes about how the fight is worth it in the long run:

> A man who gives way to his passions is like a man who is shot at by an enemy, catches the arrow in his hands, and then plunges it into his own heart. A man who is resisting his passions is like a man who is shot at by an enemy, and although the arrow hits him, it does not seriously wound him because he is wearing a breastplate. But the man who is uprooting his passions is like a man who is shot at by an enemy, but who strikes the arrow and shatters it or turns it back into his enemy's heart.[84]

So when you are faced with temptation, or when you feel tired from the fight, ask yourself which person you want to be. Do you want to be the person who is intentionally harming themselves? Do you want to be the person who is guarded? Or do you want to be the person who fights back and wins?

The first way is the easy nonresistant way, and it leads to destruction. Here you don't even bother to put up a fight, and you are left bleeding from self-inflicted pain. Although it was the enemy who attacked you with the temptation, you were the one who consciously chose to fall into the trap, and instead of escaping the temptation, you willingly took the bait and indulged in its pleasure.

---

84 Svitlana Kobets, "The Desert Fathers," accessed October 10, 2022, http://www.slavdom.com/index.php?id=88.

The second man, someone shot by the enemy but not seriously wounded, will build resiliency and sharpen his spiritual senses. In this scenario, you are wearing the breastplate of righteousness, and the enemy cannot penetrate it. You have earned that breastplate by refining yourself, avoiding temptation, and dying to your desires. You might have been wounded a few times, as any fighter would be in battle, but it has not brought you down. The enemy will never cease aiming for your destruction, but your defenses will not fail, and he cannot fatally harm you.

The last man, who is uprooting his passions, is the best fighter to imitate. Here, you become the mighty warrior who vigorously takes the attacking arrows and shatters them without a flinch. You destroy the enemy by completely breaking free from his attack, leaving him like the deplorable failure he is. You use his own weapons against him, just like when Christ was tempted in Matthew 4. Christ used the power of the Scriptures to disarm Satan, and the lies of the enemy did not deceive Him and bring Him down. The Church Fathers also tell us about other ways we can fight against the will of the flesh: praying and fasting.

Praying, and especially uttering the Jesus prayer in times of weakness, is one way to transform the posture of your heart and alter the direction of your words and actions. We are told to pray unceasingly (1 Thess. 5:17), so repeating the simple words of the Jesus prayer is a great way to do so. When a thought, an image, or ungodly words tempt you, lift your heart in prayer and audibly or inaudibly say, "Lord Jesus Christ, Son of God, have mercy on me, a sinner." Those powerful words will pierce your opponent and summon the power of the Holy Spirit in you.

Fasting also helps us fight temptation, as St. Augustine says, "Fasting purifies the soul. It lifts up the mind, and it brings the body into subjection to the spirit. It makes the heart contrite and humble, scatters the clouds of desire, puts out the flames of lust and enkindles the true light of chastity."[85] The more you can control your stomach, the more you can control your body and your will. Fasting strengthens your self-control; it is like a muscle that grows every time you control your will and turn down the food your body craves. When your self-control is stronger than your desires, you set yourself up for success when the temptations come flooding your way. And not only does self-control strengthen your spiritual life, it also improves your overall life. Scientist have found that self-control is positively related to affective well-being and life satisfaction.[86] The famous Marshmallow Test experiment reaffirms this conclusion.

In the 1960s a team of scientists led by Walter Mischel at Stanford University studied children's self-control. Preschoolers were given two options for a reward: a marshmallow they could have immediately, or two marshmallows if they waited twenty minutes for them. The study followed them into high school and adulthood and made a remarkable discovery. In high school, the children who had waited longer for their reward had higher SAT scores. And at age 27–32 they had a lower body mass index and a better sense of self-worth, pursued their goals more effectively, and coped more adaptively with frustration and stress. At midlife, those who waited had distinctively different brain scans in areas linked to addictions and obesity than those who opted for instant gratification. Delaying your gratification by utilizing self-control will benefit you

85 Carolyn Berghuis, "The Power Fasting Part I," *A Catholic Moment,* accessed October 10, 2022, https://www.acatholic.org/friday-2-12-16-the-power-fasting/.

86 Wilhelm Hofmann et al., "Yes, but Are They Happy? Effects of Trait Self-Control on Affective Well-Being and Life Satisfaction," *Journal of Personality* 82, no. 4 (June 11, 2013): 265–77, https://doi.org/10.1111/jopy.12050.

spiritually, physically, and emotionally, and will help you fight back against the temptations you will encounter.

While you are fighting back, it also helps to keep yourself occupied with holy things. If you fill your time with prayer, spiritual readings, church services, and beneficial daily obligations, you won't have idle time where the devil will find an opportune time to attack. It was in King David's idleness that the devil led him to be tempted by the woman he saw bathing on the roof. We will all certainly have some times of idleness, but when you find yourself bored and alone, don't let Satan tempt you with watching illicit entertainment. Keep your focus on the things of God, and don't let boredom derail you. You can also put practical things in place to help you avoid such content. Many software programs and apps are available to block explicit content from reaching your electronic devices. Or you can change your environment to help you resist those temptations. You can lean in on accountability and keep your bedroom door open if you live with others. You can also put limits on screentime so that you are not tempted by excessive exposure. You can place your phone in a different room before bedtime so that when you're unable to sleep, you're not tempted to reach for it and wander to harmful content.

. . . . .

There are many ways to guard yourself with the weapons God has provided you in the Scriptures. Lean on the aid of the Holy Spirit and ask Him to help you fight your battles. You are at war with an enemy who has been cunningly deceiving humans since the beginning of time, so be on guard. But do not lose hope, for the Scripture promises that "No temptation has overtaken you except such as is common to man; but God *is* faithful, who will not allow you to be tempted beyond what you are able, but with the temptation will also make the way of escape, that you may be able to bear it" (1 Cor. 10:13). There will always be a way out of the temptation in front of you, so don't be held captive by your strong urges but look for that way of escape, which God will provide. Asking for strength and grace from God will help you bear and overcome the temptation. Saint John Chrysostom comments about this verse:

> Paul implies that there must be temptations which we cannot bear. What are these? Well, all of them in effect. For the ability to bear them comes from God's grace, which we obtain by asking for it. God gives us patience and brings us speedy deliverance. In this way the temptation becomes bearable.[87]

Myths about Temptation

Myth #1: I will never overcome this temptation, so I will give up the fight.

Not every person will completely overcome their temptations. That might sound hopeless, but perfection is not the only way to measure success. While overcoming a temptation entirely and not falling into it again is the ultimate goal, fighting it round after round is another way to win against it. And with every round you'll get stronger and faster at beating it.

When I was in high school, I was part of the swimming team. Although I wasn't the best swimmer and I never won a gold medal, swimming was the highlight of my day. At each competition, the swimming coach would time my races and compare them with my previous race. If I beat my fastest time, as soon as I got out of the pool, she'd shout, "Personal best!" Every time I heard those words,

---

87   Bray, *1-2 Corinthians: Ancient Christian Commentary*, 96.

it would make me very happy. It meant that even if I didn't win the race, I still won against myself. I beat my old time and got faster, which is worth celebrating.

It's the same with temptation. For example, if you typically spend hours watching porn, and now you're down to minutes, that's a small win on your way to victory. Or if you're used to going to ungodly places several times a week and cut back to a few times a month, you're taking steps to stop the habit. Don't let the devil whisper lies and discourage you because you haven't reached perfection yet. He'll want to convince you that you'll never get over your sin and should give up. Don't give up, but keep going until you defeat that sin by the grace of God. There is purification and sanctification in the struggle.

Myth #2: I won't fit in if I'm not doing what everyone else is doing.

There is some truth to this, but it's not something to be sad about. We are not of this world and shouldn't be discouraged when the world makes us feel like outcasts. If you've ever read Leviticus, Numbers, or Deuteronomy, you'll notice a long list of commands from God on how His people should carry out their lives. Those commands were meant to set the Israelites apart from everyone else and their way of life. Similarly, we are God's chosen people, meant to be different from everyone else, and we stand out from the crowd by following His commandments.

Living differently won't be easy, and many tribulations will follow, but Christ gives us hope when He says, "In the world you will have tribulation; but be of good cheer, I have overcome the world" (John 16:33). If you find that being the odd one out is difficult, then surround yourself with others who have similar goals of godliness to help you along the journey. While growing up, having friends of the same faith helped me tremendously. Although I felt like an outsider among my peers in school, I always felt at home with my friends from church. And that helped me to not feel so isolated.

Myth #3: My temptations are not as bad as everyone else's.

We are called to pursue righteousness, but be aware of the sin of self-righteousness creeping in. Maybe you read the statistics on porn use earlier in this chapter and thought, "I don't struggle with that, so compared to what seems like the majority, I'm pretty good." If this sounds like you, don't just pat yourself on the back; thank God for His mercies and that you don't have to fight that temptation. Pornography might not be the plank in your eye, but if you look deep enough, you likely need to overcome other sins of the flesh.

Comparison is dangerous when you're comparing yourself to people you think are better than you and people you think are worse than you. The only person we should compare ourselves to is the person God wants us to be: pure and full of righteousness. Don't be like the publican who thanked God that he was not like the sinful tax collector, but be like the tax collector who, "standing afar off, would not so much as raise *his* eyes to heaven, but beat his breast, saying, 'God, be merciful to me a sinner!'" (Luke 18:13). Cry out the Jesus prayer as the tax collector did, and trust in God's faithfulness to deliver you from your sins.

10

Experiencing Repentance

If you've read the last few chapters and feel like you've made too many mistakes already and are too far gone, I encourage you to set aside any feelings of defeat and allow this chapter to help you make a fresh start. Challenge yourself to let go of any shame or guilt that holds you back from repentance and renewal. The Orthodox faith is filled with radiant examples of heroes of repentance, and you can draw strength and courage from these examples.

One such hero is St. Mary of Egypt,[88] who was chasing after her lustful desires by living a life of prostitution. One day she followed a crowd heading to a church in Jerusalem, but she encountered a mighty force that stopped her from entering the church, and she knew it was her awful sins that prevented her entry. She immediately turned to the Theotokos and offered sincere repentance, promising to turn her life around. Saint Mary of Egypt then spent over

---

88 Sophronios of Jerusalem, "Life of St Mary of Egypt," Monachos.net, accessed May 15, 2023, https://web.archive.org/web/20101230181728 /http://monachos.net/content/patristics/patristictexts/182-life-of-mary.

forty-seven years in the desert in solitude, repenting and becoming a new creation in Christ.

Another example is St. Moses the Ethiopian[89] (also referred to as St. Moses the Strong or the Black), who was known for his great physical strength and for leading a life of theft, murder, and fornication. Eventually he desired to know the true God, which led him to a monastery in the wilderness of Shiheat. There he repented of his many sins, sought the monastic life, and eventually became a guiding father to many brothers and monks until his last breath.

Also, the Samaritan woman, known as St. Photini in the Orthodox tradition,[90] would draw water from the well at the hottest time of day to avoid others because she was ashamed of her history. She had five failed marriages and was then living with a man she was not married to. Everyone judged her and put her down, but Christ went out of His way to lift her up. The day she met Christ at the well, she arrived carrying the heavy weight of shame and humiliation but left there a changed woman. The only thing she carried back was the good news of meeting the Messiah, which she immediately shared with those in her city—and thus she became known as one of the first evangelists.

These are not just stories but real examples of ordinary people who did not let their sins control them; rather, they took control over their lives and changed their ways. They made the decision to turn their backs on sin and walk toward the Cross, and they spent years repenting and fighting to abandon their desires. They fought

---

89 "Commemorations for Paona 24: Marytrydom of the Great Saint Anba Moses the Black," CopticChurch.net, accessed May 15, 2023, https://www.copticchurch.net/synaxarium/10_24.html.

90 "Martyr Photini the Samaritan Woman, her Sons, and Those with Them," The Orthodox Church in America, accessed May 3, 2024, https://www.oca.org/saints/lives/2013/03/20/100846-martyr-photini-the-samaritan-woman-her-sons-and-those-with-them.

long and hard, showing us it's possible to completely turn our lives around by the grace of God.

Metanoia

You can also draw strength from the fact that repentance (and thus forgiveness) is at the very heart of the Gospel. At the very beginning of the gospels, one of the first messages preached was the message of repentance from St. John the Baptist. His mission was to prepare the way for Christ, and he did so by urging the people to "Repent, for the kingdom of heaven is at hand!" (Matt. 3:2). He knew that the people had to change their ways and repent to be ready to receive Christ.

Because repentance is so fundamental to our Faith, Orthodox worship services are filled with symbolism, sacraments, and holy practices that reflect the process of repentance and forgiveness. Each physical practice is meant to reflect the internal state of the heart, and as our heart longs to redirect its desires in repentance, we use our hands, knees, and head to bow down in a prostration. We enter a state of metanoia with every prostration we make. Metanoia, stemming from Greek origins, is defined as a "transformative change of heart."[91] Every time we bow down in metanoia and utter, "Lord, have mercy," we change our direction, rise up, and become new. If sin is missing the mark, then repentance is a redirection to reach that mark.

Even though our Lord calls us to be perfect as our Father in heaven is perfect (Matt. 5:48), all of us have fallen short and sinned. Our mistakes shouldn't deter us from perfection; in fact, we should accept that we will sin and not be surprised when we do. Instead, that command

---

91 *Merriam-Webster*, s.v. "metanoia (n.)," accessed May 19, 2023, https://www.merriam-webster.com/dictionary/metanoia.

from Christ should encourage us to keep trying and striving toward perfection. It is through the act of getting up after each fall that we get closer to God. So be aware of the shame and guilt that can hold you back from rising up after you fall. In some cases, the shame and guilt you experience can be worse than the sin committed.

Shame and Guilt

After the pleasure of sin overtakes our senses for mere moments, it may leave us with a dark cloud of shame and guilt that follows us like an unwelcome shadow. And shame and guilt don't come alone; they're usually accompanied by regret, embarrassment, self-pity, or self-loathing. That is the dark reality of sin. Although it might look shiny and attractive on the outside, it often leads to destruction; as St. Paul says, "For the wages of sin *is* death." But he doesn't stop there; he reminds us of the hope we live by and continues, saying, "but the gift of God *is* eternal life in Christ Jesus our Lord" (Rom. 6:23).

There are two different types of guilt, however: helpful and unhelpful. While unhelpful guilt can hold us back from repentance and from moving forward in our lives as Christians, helpful guilt can actually, as you might suspect, be helpful to us. Helpful guilt shows you that you've sinned and you should consequently feel bad about that. It proves that you know right from wrong, and that the Holy Spirit in you is convicting you of the wrong you've done. The guilty feeling signals to your mind and spirit that you did something wrong and should do something to make it right. Some like to call this conviction, because helpful guilt moves you to action and correction, while unhelpful guilt does not.

Unhelpful guilt is a similar bad feeling you experience after doing that wrongful act, but instead of leading you to recourse, it traps you in those feelings. It chains your feet to the ground, keeping you fixated on the past and unable to move forward, and you can't stop thinking, "How could I have done such a great misdeed?!" You beat yourself up over whatever it was that you did and convince yourself that you are unworthy of forgiveness. This behavior can have roots in pride, thinking we are not susceptible to sin and are better than our sinful nature. We should all expect that we will fall short and sin, and while we try to avoid it, we will give in to temptation from time to time because sin still lingers in the brokenness of our humanity.

While guilt is a feeling about something you did, shame takes things to another level because it is a feeling about who you are.[92] Guilt tells you that you have sinned, but shame tells you that you are a sinner. Shame can threaten your identity by letting your mistakes define who you are. Sometimes you can even feel ashamed about something outside of your control, such as where you come from or something that has happened to you (such as abuse). If you do start feeling shame, don't let it overtake you. Do not let it linger, because it will cause you anxiety and lead to hopelessness.

While you should shut down feelings of shame immediately, you can allow guilty feelings to be warning lights, cautioning you to redirect your path. For some, God sends undeniable warning lights, like the blinding light St. Paul got struck with before he became a follower of Christ (Acts 9:3–9), the storm at sea Jonah was thrown into before getting swallowed by the fish (Jon. 1:15–17), or the rooster crowing three times after St. Peter denied Christ (Luke 22:54–62). Scripture points out that there are two options when we are facing regrettable circumstances, "For godly sorrow produces repentance *leading* to salvation, not to be regretted; but the sorrow

---

92   Peter Bouteneff, *How to Be a Sinner* (Yonkers, NY: St Vladimir's Seminary Press, 2018), 109.

of the world produces death" (2 Cor. 7:10). These faith heroes all could have become completely overwhelmed by their sin and weighed down by guilt and shame—like Judas, to his death—but they chose to turn and repent. They were among many conquerors who bravely embraced repentance.

Making All Things New

There is an undeniable power that repentance and confession have over sin, as the sacrament carries a mighty force that loosens the grip of sin. I've seen this evidence of God's sweet redemption in my own life and in the lives of so many other people I'm blessed to know, like Stacey. Stacey was a girl I once served in youth ministry when she was a teenager. As the church teachers taught the youth about purity, Stacey was not on the same page. She bought into the lies of the world and believed that sex wasn't as big of a deal as her church was making it out to be. She had a carefree attitude toward sex, and despite my reasoning with her and telling her everything I'm telling you in this book, she had her mind made up. She admitted honestly that if presented with the opportunity to have sex, she would most likely take it. Her curiosity was steering the ship, and there was no room on board for self-control and long-term vision.

A few years later, Stacey became a beautiful young woman and started hanging out with the wrong crowd that negatively influenced her, and she wanted to indulge her sexual curiosity. She met a man who enticed her, and she ended up sleeping with him. Almost immediately after this happened, he left her, and she was devastated, heartbroken, and angry. In hindsight, she understood that he was only using her to get what he wanted. She learned her lesson the hard way, but thankfully that didn't leave her spiraling into what could have been a vicious cycle. She learned quickly from that burn that the fire of sexual passion was dangerous. But that lesson wasn't a cheap one to learn. It cost her her virginity and derailed her purity.

It took hard work and many meetings with her father confessor and her therapist to move forward from the life she wanted to leave behind. She fought off shame and guilt to be able to live in the present and not remain stuck in the past. She changed the crowd she was hanging out with and surrounded herself with God-fearing friends who strived to live purely despite the social pressures around them. She dreads having to have that serious conversation with a potential future spouse about her past and where that might lead the relationship; nonetheless, God's grace and redemption are unquestionable and will carry her through it. Her repentance and confession, with God's forgiveness, have made her new.

So no matter where your sexual desires have led you and what physical boundaries you've crossed, remember there is always a way back to God. Whether you've made a few mistakes in your dating life or too many to count, repentance is still within reach. Even if you have dated someone who took you farther from Christ, you are never too far gone to return. Or if hatred is in your heart over a bad breakup, God can redeem those feelings and heal your heart.

Sometimes God allows us to go through storms and hard times for our benefit, even though it might have been our actions that led us there. He gives us the opportunities to learn from our mistakes. I've met young people disappointed by how they handled a relationship or treated someone. While they only see how badly they messed up, I see growth. The fact that they can recognize where they went wrong shows me how honest they're being with themselves. Apologizing and owning up to their mistakes with their previous partner offers a chance at mature reconciliation. Whether they end up back together or not, their willingness to do better next time will make all the difference in their next relationship.

Admitting our mistakes and handing them over to God will allow for restoration in our relationship with Him. Look at how compassionate the Lord was with someone like the Prodigal Son. In that story, we see a son convinced that he would never be satisfied in his father's house, so he leaves, seeking to satisfy his desires (Luke 15:11–32). But when he hits rock bottom, he sits and reflects on his life. He recognizes his mistakes and decides to do something about them, so he makes a plan to go back to his father's house. He knows what he wants to say to seek his father's forgiveness. Upon returning home, his father embraces him, covers him with precious gifts, and has a feast to celebrate his son's return.

The Lord eagerly awaits you to return to Him as the Prodigal Son did, so you must be honest with yourself and reflect on your mistakes, and make a plan to get back on the right path. And don't let anything get in the way of executing your plan! You'll see that God is faithful to forgive and always longs for you to return home.

Myths about Repentance and Forgiveness

Myth #1: God can't possibly forgive what I've done.

There are many lies Satan likes to make you believe are truths, and this is one of the most dangerous ones because if he can keep you stuck in shame and guilt, you will never move toward repentance and renewal. You'll stay hopeless, feeling like God's love is out of reach. Whenever you start feeling like that, remember the words of St. Paul and the real truth he shares: "that you, being rooted and grounded in love, may be able to comprehend with all the saints what *is* the width and length and depth and height—to know the love of Christ which passes knowledge; that you may be filled with all the fullness of God" (Eph. 3:17–19). God's love for us is endless, in every direction!

No one in the Bible who genuinely sought repentance was ever turned away. Not one saint who diligently chose to turn their life around was ever denied a holy life. Neither will you be rejected if you seek God's forgiveness. So don't let any lies fill your mind and deter you from the way back to God. Search the Scripture for God's truth; it will prove to be the lifeline you desperately need to become new.

Myth # 2: I've ruined my chance at a good relationship because of my past.

Too many young people think they've lost their chance at a good relationship because of past sinful mistakes. Whether they intended to indulge in their sexual desire or fell to the pressure of a partner, they believe that their regrettable actions will follow them into every relationship. But we have seen in this book that this doesn't have to be the case.

Every person has the chance to turn a new page on their lives through the power and healing mystery of repentance and confession. And for some, healing from past traumatic experiences might require working with a therapist. We live in an age where we are learning more about mental health and how different resources can be helpful, and we have learned that although our experiences shape us, they don't have to define us. We can challenge our mentality and change the narrative we tell ourselves; we can turn a bad experience into a valuable lesson.

And it helps to remember that the past is in the past. You don't have to live in it. Live in the present and move forward toward the future. It is not healthy to look back at the sins that brought destruction to your life. We're warned in Luke 17:32 to "remember Lot's wife," she looked back, longing for the life she had lived in Sodom and Gomorrah and was immediately turned into a pillar of salt, as God had warned her. While reflecting on and learning from mistakes is beneficial, excessively dwelling on them is not helpful to moving forward. Dwell on them long enough so that it will lead you to repentance, and then trust that God has forgiven you, that you no longer need to live in shame and guilt. Forgive yourself also.

Myth #3: I've kept myself pure, so I can't accept anyone who isn't pure.

This myth is the opposite of the previous one. You might have a clean past and have never crossed any sexual lines. Therefore, thoughts of a self-righteousness nature start filling your mind, and you might think you're off limits to potential partners with a sexual past. While you have a right to choose who you end up with—and their past might be a deciding factor—it is not right to judge others. Never underestimate how God can change someone's heart, despite their past experiences.

Be careful also how you label certain sins. For example, a woman might have lost her virginity, but a man who is a virgin but looks at pornography might think he's pure when in fact, he is not. A guy might have dated multiple women with whom he kept pure relationships, but a girl might have been in one relationship where she mistreated her partner. In this case, the girl thinks she's better because she doesn't have a history of multiple relationships—but she is not. And remember, someone's exposed sins might be bad, but your hidden sins might be worse.

I once received an email from a concerned young man. He told me he was engaged to a beautiful woman, inside and out, with all the qualities he sought in a wife. They shared the same values and were heading toward the same goals. But there was one thing troubling him. She'd had multiple sexual partners in the past. It had been years since she lived that lifestyle and she had done the hard work of repenting and confessing. Yet the consequences of her past seemed to come up again when her fiancé felt that their wedding night might be less special or that issues might come up in their marital sex life.

I wrote back and told him that it was normal to have these concerns but that he had to fight through them if he wanted to continue in the relationship. He had to fully accept her repentance and not hold her past against her. If issues rose up later in their marriage, they would have to be willing to work on them. Ultimately, he had to decide if his relationship with her was worth fighting through these obstacles. He assured me that it was. In turn, his care for her and willingness to navigate this hurdle made him the right partner for her.

Surrender your life to God and fully submit to Him, and He will guide you into the right relationship. He will bring you the right person, and even if you or your partner have a past, you'll be able to handle it by His grace. Allow forgiveness to be the lens you see others through and not self-righteousness.

CONCLUSION

Waiting and dating are important journeys anyone considering marriage must go through. Each person's journey will be different from another's. Their struggles, losses, and victories will be unique to them. Their timeline and milestones will be different. And their walk with God through the journey will shape them.

Whether you've been patiently enduring a season of waiting or have experienced a cycle of dating, I hope this book has offered guidance on the issues you're facing. I pray it has given you the right tools for you to move forward where you feel stuck. At the very least, I hope it expanded your knowledge of godly relationships.

Remember that your growth in relationships doesn't have a finish line; it is a work in progress. If you want to learn more about marriage, there are plenty of books, podcasts, sermons, blogs, and many more resources you can get your hands on (some of which I have referenced in this book). If you discern that God's will for you is to live a life of singleness, then dive into resources on that.

And don't embark on these journeys alone. Immerse yourself in a thriving community that will help you swim through any rough waters you encounter. Surround yourself with people who will be there to throw you a life jacket or pull you out of the water if needed. Get closer to God, who will be your ultimate captain, guiding you on your path. He will lead you through storms until you reach calm shores. He will provide U-turns and ways of escape when you find yourself in too deep. He wants to lead you to His Kingdom, whether single or with a partner He has prepared for you. You must be willing to do the hard work of swimming upstream into unknown territories, moving one arm after the other without always knowing where it leads. All in all, live by these verses, and all will be well:

Trust in the LORD with all your heart,
And lean not on your own understanding;
In all your ways acknowledge Him,
And He shall direct your paths. (Proverbs 3:5–6)

ABOUT THE AUTHOR

Lilyan Andrews is a certified life coach with a focus on relationships, and she is an engineer, speaker, and blogger as well. Through her coaching and writing she aims to help Christian youth navigate the complexities of singleness and dating. She lives in Stony Point, NY with her husband Rev. Dr. Antony Andrews and their three daughters, where she serves alongside him at Virgin Mary and St. Pachomius Coptic Orthodox Church.

ACKNOWLEDGMENTS

While my name is on the cover of this book, I could not have done it without the support of my loving village—the group of people God has put in my life to enrich it.

To my wonderful husband, Fr. Antony Andrews: Thank you for your endless support and for believing in me when sometimes I didn't believe in myself. For pushing me to see God's plan for this book before it became a reality. For sacrificing what little free time you have to help me in any way I needed. You are the strength of our home, and the girls and I are blessed to have you.

To my parents and in-laws, Nadia and Youssef Estafanous, and Elham and Erian Andrews: Thank you for raising us in a steadfast faith and struggling with us as we grew into the adults we've become. I'll be forever grateful for your encouragement and long hours of babysitting. I could not have done it without your support and willingness to help almost any hour of the day.

To the various Coptic Orthodox parishes I've been a part of: Thank you for creating a beautiful and rich environment to grow up in. For the deep faith that you teach and cherish. For fruitful communities, wonderful mentors, and the safe space you provide. I can only try to serve others and do for them what my youth leaders have done for me. I'll spend the rest of my life trying to pay back all that I've gained from your love.

To all my dedicated readers: Thank you for reading my blog when it was just a fresh new idea and being with me from day one. For your heartfelt messages about how God was using my humble writing in your life. For your encouragement to keep writing. You are the main reason I am here and have an audience for this book.

To all those who had active hands in reading, providing feedback, and making this book better, especially Sherry Sourial: The time you sacrificed to help me with this project will never be forgotten. Your willingness to read every word I wrote with enthusiasm, including editing all my blog posts, was the exact support I needed.

To the team at Ancient Faith Publishing: Marci Johnson, Donna Ryan, Ellie Shackelford Bernasol, Samuel Heble, Elijah Sabourin, and Melinda Johnson, and to Dr. Roxanne Louh and Fr. Paul Hodge for reviewing the book. It has been a dream to work with you all. Your valuable input and tremendous efforts have made the book into what it is today. The amount of care you showed with every suggestion and direction you provided is more than I could have hoped for.

Finally, to my Lord and Master: I pray that this book delivers the message of Your words and not just mine. I pray You allow it to reach those who need it. Thank You for blessing me with the time, energy, words, and all the resources I needed to write this book, and for allowing my love for You to grow even fonder through this experience. You've given me a life full of trials and triumphs: trials to refine me and triumphs to let Your glory shine through. Many trials came during the writing of this book, but I pray it turns into a triumph. So here's to a lifetime full of trials and triumphs! I can't wait to see what You have next for me.

Let's Connect!

Lilyan Andrews would love to connect with you on Instagram, **@LilyanAndrews** or on her website, **LilyanAndrews.com**. If you've enjoyed reading this book, let others know about it by posting on social media and tagging Lilyan, and leave a review on the Ancient Faith Store website through the QR link below.

We hope you have enjoyed and benefited from this book. Your financial support makes it possible to continue our nonprofit ministry both in print and online. Because the proceeds from our book sales only partially cover the costs of operating **Ancient Faith Publishing** and **Ancient Faith Radio**, we greatly appreciate the generosity of our readers and listeners. Donations are tax deductible and can be made at **www.ancientfaith.com.**

To view our other publications,
please visit our website:
store.ancientfaith.com

 **ANCIENT FAITH RADIO**

Bringing you Orthodox Christian music, readings, prayers, teaching, and podcasts 24 hours a day since 2004 at **www.ancientfaith.com**